Books on Demand

Gerhard Vohs

Cat Tommy
Kidnapping with results

**A charming history
about the readiness,
for his cat
to do everything**

Photo: Gerhard Vohs »cat of Tommy«

Bibliographic information of the German national library:

The German national library registers this publication in the German national bibliography; specified bibliographic data are retrievable on the Internet about http://dnb.dnb.de.

Production and publishing company: BoD – Books on Demand, Norderstedt, Germany

ISBN: 978-3-7357-2232-4

Table of contents:

1. From master's view

2. From Tom's micron view

Cat Tommy
Kidnapping with results.
1. From master's view

1.1 Welcome Tommy

It was spring a few years ago when the cat of my friend Marc got boy. Three absolutely blind, deaf and absolutely helpless European short hair cat's babies saw the light of the world. I particularly noticed a cat with cinnamon-colored drawing. She had been drilled through with their little head and the tiny front paws between her siblings to find a warm and safe place to mums breast.

Easily with a finger I stroked the fur and already I heard a high onomatopoeic sound, a squeaking one hiss. They are still so small and unassailable and are busy in their initial life mainly to sleep and sucking on mom's chest.

Days later, they opened the eyes and up to now only by smell and touch oriented kittens, now could see her siblings and her mother. At that time the eyes see still cloudy and blue, but that changed in the next few days.

I watched the little cinnamon cat. She played with her tail. Again and again they tried to capture him and when I stroked it, she arched her back, to feel the touch of my finger intense. Then she began to purr and because it had happened to me. I had fallen in love with this cat and she wanted to have.

»Loris was identified right from the start for you«, spoke Marc to me. »You should call them on occasion with the name, so that it is already accustomed herself to it and also is trusted with your voice.«

Lori what a funny name, sounds like Dorte, a mix between kebab and pie. But cats do not care what name they are addressed. The main thing to vote the number of treats.

"In four weeks then it is old enough to say goodbye, then I'll bring it over to you."

Two days later I was back, watching my future new roommate, as she leapt her sleeping mother, who then snarling manner had the lists.

When I called them and caused with the fingertips rubbing bruits, it came curiously, sniffed and turned round. Besides, she made a hump and pressed this to the snapping hand, a request to fondle. Feelings of happiness flowed through to my body, one moment which cannot be caught in words.

Over and over again I stroked from the head up to the tail her fur, over and over again it prodded with the head my stroking hand in.

»Go on, do not stop,« she gave me to understand it, and so I let go of her only when she had had enough.

The next day I spent in a pet store, looking for a bed, a litter box, after toys, feeding bowls, flea collar with a bell, and of course for food for my diva. Here I was standing in front of a full meter long shelf with cat food as a noise barrier dampened the noise.

There was ragout, salmon and chicken with potatoes and thistle oil, beef with Italian ham, lamb and beef with natural rice and wheat germ oil, game and fowl with whole meal pasta and linseed oil, beef with potato and black cumin oil, sheep and fowl with natural rice and hempseed oil.

I collected myself to the head and thought only what there would be, nevertheless, for tasty things for cats. While I push a pizza with ham and pineapple in the oven, cultured cats can refresh themselves healthy and pacifistic in the foods like lamb, game, sheep and fowl.

A modern, uncomplicated, healthy and balanced food based on natural ingredients, I took the labels. A guaranteed vitamin-rich whole food that has been carefully prepared and carefully by experts.

Twenty aluminum bowls and twenty sachets from different manufacturers I took, and some cans. In addition still some bags dry food, a comfortable cozy bed with lowered entry, stable edge and removable reversible cushion, as well as toys, litter box, bowls and a collar. At the checkout I then delighted me about the peppered total that put me almost faint.

Fully loaded I went home and put everything first in the hallway. I had to think about where I'm doing all the stuff back and could as I do my little new friend cozy. The bed comes into the bedroom, the cat litter box into the bathroom, toys distributed to the living room and for the dry food, jars and bowls I had only times evacuate a full cupboard empty.

I had not bought a cat tree, because it will be difficult to hold a cat in the flat if one lives in a detached house. The first time will be my 160 square meters flat a place of residence to be explored and then I will accustom them slowly to my garden where she can use the tree for sharpening of her claws.

Tomorrow is the day where my small Lori enters and I hope that they like in her new environment will find. In the neighborhood there are some cats with whom she can close friendship and go hunting together. However, in the evening, before the nightfall it should already be a home. Earlier my mother had also said always: Boy if the street lanterns begin, you have to be at home. I hope that Lori also understands this.

The next day came, a Saturday. Marc appeared late afternoon with his wife Denise and my new occupant. Shyness she lay in the cat's basket, might not move. Fear and horror spread with her because she did not know what happened with her.

"We put the basket here open into the hallway and then let them come out on their own. Cats are curious. She'll come out. It's best to put on here said opening a used piece of clothing, then she takes your talk smells was that they actually should already know, when you had them petted. Then it all seems a bit sensitive to it. "

I went to the bathroom and got a used T-shirt out of the laundry basket and put it down in front of the cat basket. Then I went with Marc and Denise in the basement of my home bar to only times to let my new roommate a little alone.

Curiosity grabbed me when I went from the basement to the kitchen. I carefully looked around the corner to see if it is still in the basket. She was still there, had moved no piece, seemed obviously also tired, his eyes fell to her again and again.

"She's still in her basket," I said when I walked into the basement again.

»Speaking of "them," we were yesterday at the veterinarian and have had to examine the kitten; everything is OK, except for a small incident.«

»Well, I hope sometimes nothing serious,« I mentioned.

»Not really, it is still only a small misinterpretation, a slight genetic mutation, only a slight misinterpretation. It's like the mistake to ever understand a woman or how the classification of the directives to the left and right.«

»Instep me thus on the torture what is with the cat she is ill, does she suffer from what, does she have complaints or some other concomitants? Must she take drugs to influence the disease course or what is wrong?«

»No, no nothing of all there, they are completely healthy! It is only one misunderstanding, a provided, a sex-specified mistake, the categorization in a wrong group.«

»What wrong group, what mistake, I understand only railway station. Can you express yourself sometimes a little bit clearer that also normal people understand you?«

»Now if one compared the cat to a person, she could pee after the newest knowledge in the standing position what means that the name Loris is inappropriate, because the cat's lady is a tomcat.«

»Oh, Ups …, one had bought no pink little bed well that I. But, nevertheless, this makes no difference shit, whether lady cat or tomcat. What do you make for a fuss from it or you mean I give them so again?«

I raised my right hand, clenched them to the fist, rolled out the forefinger and bumped several times against my forehead. Then I contrived the names Tommy and welcomed them, no him, on a new in his new home.

Fairly long time later packed me once more the curiosity and thus I went to the hall to look what is with the small rascal. The basket was empty. The small elegant being had ventured in the pit of the lion, had broken off all bridge behind itself and now was to be got to know on discovery tour around his sphere to settle in it. Thus I put away the basket and sneaked away carefully not to frighten him, all the same where he just was.

When I went to bed, I left open all doors, so that he could move cheerfully everywhere there and the next morning I looked for the moment after his feeding bowls. He had eaten what calmed me a little. However, a peculiar odor rose to me in the nose when I entered the sitting room. I did research after the cause of this evaporation and found a small lake in the corner. Tommy had peed there.

Shit, I thought. Nevertheless, has really forgotten him to show his loo. Thus I went on the search to see whether he had still cultivated other "loos". Then I suddenly saw under the curtain a small pink-colored nose and two eyes looking out. Indiscernibly I approached him, on the knee sliding, laid the head to ground. With the finger at the head which moved mincing to and fro I received his full attention. Quick as a flash one of his paws twitched under the process out and tried to my fingers catch.

When I was close enough with him, I lay down level on the ground, I allowed to play him still for a while with my finger, before I took him under the curtain out, laid him in my crook of the arm and fondled his belly quite softly. Immediately he caught in to purr, closed the eyes to slit and, besides, was to be fallen asleep near. A bond of trust developed just between Tommy and me, a bridge that started to harden indiscernibly.

Still his belly doing the crawl I went to the bathroom and put him in the cat's loo. Sniffing and with purring bruits he examined the white high-class cinder which was developed especially for the needs of a cat and provides with her fine pored surface for a pleasant dry place of the relaxation.

Then he went moment where he to the squat and let arise a bruit that strongly reminds of an artificial irrigation of regional products. I was contented and left alone him, rather looked after the blotch in the sitting room.

As one of its own kind I moved on all fours in order to remove the stain in the corner. A reason for Tommy, me constantly jumping in the heels. So I left everything and only times and occupied myself with the ever trusting becoming hangover.

After well one hour he was so tired that he has fallen asleep directly with the play. Carefully I picked up him and laid him in his little bed, stroked him warily what he accepted purring.

Suddenly one rang in the door. Tommy tore open the eyes, jumped out of the bed and crept away behind the sofa. A sound what he did not know yet and seemed menacing for him.

I gave up him, went to the door, opened them and one of my neighbors stood before it. A visit every Sunday, it should be to bridge the boredom of a single person by chatting unimportant things; to chat easily about God and the world, about women, cars and other things; on the airs and graces of fellow quirks of colleagues; on the affectation of the pretty waitress from the village inn.

»Hey, walk in, however, is careful where you step there, I have because a small hangover to the sublease, had brought Marc yesterday.«

We went down to the basement bar, opened us a beer and met with my new housemates to. After a while he asked:

»Where is then the cat, I would see them with pleasure sometimes.«

»She knew that you come and fear has agreed. No no that has so got a fright by the ring that she has crept away behind the sofa. If she comes out after there, I show them to you, quite a sweet guy.«

While my neighbor was standing in front of the counter and I behind, we talked about very trivial things. Suddenly I felt a slight stinging at my heel, like the pricking needle in acupuncture. Without interrupting my conversation, I lifted my leg, scratching at the heel and put it down again. A short time later, I again felt like trying to pin my heel to penetrate.

I looked down and immediately it became clear to me who was responsible for the traditional Chinese medicine.

My small scamp tried to bite with his small mouth in my heel. I could not describe the luck at all that I felt all at once when I picked up him and put on the bar. Eleven stairs he has ventured down to find me, his master.

»This is Tommy, my new occupant,« told I my neighbor. »Yesterday come and today already man in the house.«

We did not know ourselves yet long and, nevertheless, I suddenly had the feeling that it would have to be longer already much and how much I enjoy, nevertheless, the suture of Tommy. Yesterday come and today already a part of my life what will bring and there still the future everything.

1.2 The lout's years begin

Weeks and months passed. Tommy grew up meanwhile into a confessed cat, to a right small tyrant to whom nothing threw off course so easily. It was a very intelligent cat, learnt fast, particularly when he could use the learnt to his advantage.

When I wake up, he stood so long outside the bathroom until I showered fresh, shaved and dressed again get out. Then I had only once filled his food bowls. Not that he was hungry, no, they had to be filled only easy to know because what if one was hungry. Then a short sniff his eatables, inhaling the aroma and going to the terrace door.

From there I hear every morning the pathetic meow of a cat who would like to go for her early morning walk particularly the toilet duct in neighbor garden on the freshly hacked, broken up patch fragrantly smelling of earth.

Actually, Tommy should remain only on my property, however, arbitrarily he had expanded his catchment area on and on what encloses meanwhile at least fifteen properties in every sky direction.

Thus he creeps for the moment about the partition wall to the neighbor to fetch his ration Brekkies to himself there. Then after various additional strokes because he receives nobody else it further goes to the next property where the next meal waited for him. Also here an extensive back massage rounds the second breakfast, his most full satisfaction.

Food makes Tired and thus a nap is held before the third breakfast for the moment in the Hollywood swing of the neighbor located behind it. Older man who had made his sports the hobby and he exercised the sport only in very special disciplines in which he bred homing pigeons. He has made it action-objective that Tommy looks at his homing pigeons as not hunting-worth objects and the pigeons dare even with her typical head motion along him, without Tommy the water in the mouth gathers.

Homing pigeons were earlier the ultimate kick to dispatch news. Everywhere they flew by the air, to distributed communications, messages, letters and letters. Every household disposed of such a flying object, of a maritime predecessor of the post.

However, they kept themselves not long, because there was less and less letter pigeon breeder. No miracle, because the geriatric average of a breeder lies with sixty years and therefore beyond the reproductive age.

Today where all over the country mobile phones are used to satisfy the gossip need of many people, an SMS is faster written, than a rolled up slip of paper which is fastened in a container on the foot of a pigeon.

After Tommy had held extensively his midday nap, then it goes on, because there still the other neighbors who provided for the main dish were for his midday food.

I was surprised the first time at it, why I had to throw away so much from his little eater. Besides, I had changed the kinds constantly and also continuously the manufacturers. However, no matter whether Whiskas, Felix, Kite Kat, Sheba, royal Canine or other genus brands, he grumbled in the morning so long around to his bowls were filled which landed then in the evening dried in the garbage tonne.

Big worries I came along, checked up him of the doctor, however, he suffered neither from bulimia, nor was his body skeleton-like. He was completely healthy, built hard, well nourished, and not was active too thickly and sportily.

However, one day I received a phone call, the phone call of a woman from the closer neighborhood:

»Do they miss, actually, her cat Tommy?«

Tommy carries a neckband with an address follower to distinguish him as a free running cat from a without man one.

»No, not really. In the morning he always takes to the road and mostly comes about afternoon again home. I hope he has broken nothing with you?«

»No this not! He comes since some time every day to me and lets cook from me, a while on the sofa sleeps and then disappears again.«

»Now also understand I, why he eats here nothing if he fills to himself with them the paunch. From other neighbors I have heard in similar manner the same one.«

This reminds me of my childhood, as mommy had always cooked, with fresh ingredients and without any taste amplifier, however, best of all it has tasted with granny. Nevertheless, here I always had to weep to me a reason to contrived, so that granny could always say:

»But, nevertheless, you must not cry - come, I make them a little worry soup.«

Yes and then she cooked, cooked with Maggie seasoning, a taste I however, thus might.

For Tommy there were in the future only strongly diminished servings, half in the morning and the other helping if Mr. Hangover is in habit to come hungry home.

One day I stood before the terrace door and did not trust to my eyes. It was the time where Tommy came home, however, this time he did not come alone. In the towrope there were two other cats. A black / whiteness striped cat, medium-sized with small ear paintbrush and almost round head; the other an especially big, hard built cat with short thick grey fur and big far apart lying eyes.

These were very cultivated animals, one saw this, came certainly from a household here nearby. Immediately one caught in itself the mouth to clean, as if she saw just in the reflector that she would still have to get dressed up.

The ego is raised by a cultivated expression, because one is found more nicely, more elegantly and more glamorously, and thus itself the occurrence of female sexes changes towards male drastically.

Besides, the other cat was to be marked the district, while she peed in the flowerbed. One knows district marks also from the people where women give to her men a simple cheek kiss which signals that other women have no chance with the marked man.

While two stopped before the terrace, Tommy came up to me and caught in to miaow. Questioning, requesting and, nevertheless, at the same time a demanding meow. I understood his concern, he had brought friends and had invited them to food, to a dinner, to a banquet, to a gala dinner.

I went in the kitchen and Tommy ran with upraised tail before me. With an examining look he made sure of every few meters whether I also followed to his request. Come I sounded out for the moment the stock of his cat's feed, picked out the tastiest courts, because, finally, he should not disgrace himself.

Could well imagine that he had already enjoyed the cuisine of his buddies enough and now he was chosen, but to reciprocate times.

The menu plan existed of salmon and clod in fine marinade; duck and turkey in cheese sauce; beef in tomato jelly, as well as a dry fodder nibble mix beach fun and crisp menu with fish.

On a big tablet I served to the three ones five ways menu, withdrew immediately and observed from sure distance the foods of the taste illiterates.

They are very similar to us people in many respects, eat only what they know and are unreceptive to new culinary impressions.

Unfortunately, one cannot recognize from wide one whether it concerns female or male cats. Maybe it is a date, a Blind date, an anonymous establishment of contact to a common meeting; or, however, in addition anyhow one is a date, too much. Indeed, the third in practice always for different reasons seems automatic, as for example the laughing if two argue. Towards him one says again that all good things three is away are able or which comes every evil too third, like alcohol at the wheel, driving license, penalty or separation, maintenance, house broken.

Such a date is embarrassing only if one after a Ziva David from look holds and an older lady appears. This mostly lies with the profile search on the Internet where together with zip code filter and geriatric filter can be searched fast for young hares, however, one lands as fast with the girl of the 80th final-year class which even then nobody wanted to have.

When three had eaten to an end, half stayed behind in the dished plates. My mother had always said earlier:

»Eat your plate, otherwise tomorrow the sun will not!«

Yes and what do we have today of it? Climate warming and thick children.

They caught in themselves to clean what is not called that they would have made a mess. Although they do not like water, actually, at all, cats are very cleanly animals by which the concept "Cat's laundry" passes quite far the truth. If they are occupied not exactly with the food, sleeping, plays, hunting, it is cleaned.

Tommy miaowed what could be called so much like thanks, but also:

»It was good and plentiful, however, could have been better and more.«

Then everybody disappeared three.

»I will provide the next spot for the fact which still candles are lighted, accompanies from decorative red roses, a musical priming coat with the meow to Bolivian Abyssinian's cats and a cleverly arranged sundown,« I shouted to him behind. However, they all were already except reach.

Thus I cleared the perfect dinner what was not so perfect for Tommy, well.

1.3 Catnapping

One day when I came home, a white pickup van stood on the corner before my house, without label, however, with local-engaged stigmata. His scratches and bagging in the rear fender allowed to indicate at various parking attempts, particularly the broken indicator glass. A man dressed with white smock put just a box in the loading bay. I supposed a veterinarian's visit with the dog of my neighbor. A basset, a small, massive little animal at the sedate old person to run with the manner so little as possible.

He is a gentle and good-natured dog and if one says to him: "sits", then he would sit in fourteen days still at the same place if one did not lift the order before.

Not further paying attention I went to the house and how every time my first duct was to the terrace door to let in Tommy.

Today he was not there, this is not the special which passed on occasion sometimes if he sleeps somewhere in the neighborhood or otherwise occupy is. Because he is friends with every neighbor closely, even with those I knew personally not sometimes, I needed to give myself no troubles if he is late sometimes.

Thus I waited. It became evening and he was not yet at home. I became bit by bit impatient, tried to call him with delicacies as well as to lure with the bruits of a can opener. The hearing of a cat far to the human one it is real consider and even distant signals can be localized by cats substantially better.

However, this time he must probably have expanded his catchment area so far that he could not perceive my voice any more. On the other hand ...,

I called my neighbor: »Hey here is Gerard, I had seen that the veterinarian was at midday today with you. I hope that nothing is of seriousness with the dog.«

»How do you get on that the veterinarian was with me?«

»Nevertheless, I had seen the man in the smock with the transport box which stood a little piece further beside your house.«

»One with me was no veterinarian, maybe with Mrs. Helms because of those of her cat.«

I called with Mrs. Helms, but also there no veterinarian attended. They reported that one heard since some time that over and over again cats disappear here from the area that even the old clothes baskets are sprayed with scents around with it cats to attract, to catch and to sell to research laboratories that even the color of the baskets provides already about that information where a dog or a cat lives.

Panic fear packed me, fear that a cat's catcher my Tommy had caught and in a village where big-city atmosphere and criminal activity had left up to now no tracks.

Suddenly a telephone call came to me by the head that I had led about one week ago. A survey with regard to domestic animals after which the questioning in the kind, the old person and the eating habits limited itself. To the thanks one would hand over to me something in cat's feed.

Was the telephone call a spotting for a planned criminal offence? Or was it real only the questioning of a famous manufacturer, as well as me the lady this got to believe? I had not still received the promised cat's feed to date.

Cursing with terms of abuse and swearwords, accompanied by gesticulation and stomp feet, I tried to lend my fury to expression. My head got a discoloration between Red and blue which supports neck as if a plastic cuff the nape vertebras, the veins along the temple clearly came out and the artery extended, as if the blood was led away by the heart.

I could miss to myself a clyster to answer so silly questions on the phone. What I am, nevertheless, for an idiot!

If I faced now one of these cat's catchers, I would not be sorry sometimes if I had pure coincidentally just a pitchfork in the hand.

Why was I so goofy only and have answered the hypocritical questions? The phone number was suppressed, nevertheless, a sign one had to hide what. But they are clever, work like at a flirtation stock exchange, with the enticing voice of a woman and the reality can hardly keep up with the utopia.

Immediately I called my friend Marc, reported to him about my supposition and which I would have to undertake something.

»What want you to undertake? You can go only to the police and make a penal application, however, to proofs you are not able to do this. Maybe Tommy has fallen asleep only somewhere or has locked up himself in a foreign house. Vantage point till tomorrow, then he will be there absolutely again gladly and cheerfully.«

»I know that Tommy was kidnapped, I feel this. I know that he misses me that he longs for me. From tomorrow I will take vacation and search all streets, for this transporter. I know exactly like he looks and if I have found him, I replied mercy to him God,« Marc.

A terrible evening broke for me and I caught to our casualness to miss. In this time he always was at home, overnight stayed never away, in the morning maybe one, twice, but then he lay asleep on the posters of the garden chairs.

If we were tired, we went to bed together. He had his own pillow and especially at night if he stretched himself in all directions, besides, hit over and over again against my head, nevertheless, I was glad about his suture.

First I did not want at all that he comes to the bedroom, however, the guy hid on time behind the full-length border of a cocktail armchair and waited to him of the opinion I was has fallen asleep. Then with a light hardly perceptible jump on the cap not to wake up me he sat down first in the foot area of the bed. In the course of the night, nevertheless, he walked bit by bit higher, until he had reached the pillow. Here he could loll about in all directions and press his paws to me over and over again in the face.

I remained the whole night awake, looked

constantly at the terrace, however, from Tommy no track. The morning began and I waited. Then I called my boss and lied him before not to have eaten great fish and now the toilet could hardly leave.

Then I drove off to look for these transporters. It was like the infamous one looks for the needle in a haystack. Here experience is asked to recognize results without going for hours only in the area. However, how one should find a vehicle, in a time where even the smoker by his vehicle goes to the machine to buy cigarettes.

About midday I went again after to see whether Tommy waited, in the meantime, at home, however, dead loss. Again I stood on the terrace and shouted, clattered with Brekkies, with the can opener, however, nothing happened.

Marc the terrace stair came up what a little comforting tuned me.

»Hi, Gerard. Today I have made early end, nevertheless, cannot see like you torments yourself. If you were at the police,« he asked me.

»No, they should be contacts for all theft offences, also for animal theft, however, such crimes are not taken seriously by the police officers, particularly as one has also no usable and pertinent tips. There start looking I me rather itself and blow, I find one of these guys.«

»Already about that thought that it could concern an occasional theft where one waits at searching announcements in newspapers and on tree posters to bring back the cat then beaming with delight and to collect a finder's reward or to blackmail a sum?«

»You do not think one, this, nevertheless, in serious. Extortion? Kidnapping with animals, ransom demand? Who arises then thus a crazy idea?«

»However, no notion, has already seemed. There are race animals which cost a property and if run unattended around, it is a light prey for the blackmailer.«

»If you know, yesterday I have read on the Internet that more than hundred million animals every year are abused for bioassays. Many animals die during the experiments or afterwards are killed. If you have time, you can go, I want to look immediately again off, for this transporter.«

»Where want you to search him? There are certainly thousands of transporters and above all white ones.«

»He is not only white, he also has a damaged tail light and some bagging in the rear. Not sometimes motoring the criminals are able.«

We drove off, wore out all streets, lanes and ways, and could not be concurrent of course at all places, because while we looked in the north, the transporter could be in the south of the village. Still I was confident, wanted to have at all costs my hangover again.

It was slowly getting dark and in the course of the dusk the street lanterns intervened and lighted up the footpaths and roadways. In the flats the brightness shone by the windows; traffic lights changed fast from green on Red if one got closer to them; shops allowed to illuminate her neon lights and Rush Hour, with her countless floodlights, caught in to dazzle.

On the high street traffic was like in a city. Hectically the drivers from A after B moved. Then the peaceful, obliging, winning motorcyclists who ignore all speed limitations as well as cyclists those of the opinion are also to be allowed to drive without engine on the second track.

Occasionally the pedestrians who stand on half a way on the street and do not get on.

I left the high street, nowhere concentrated rather upon sideways, nevertheless a white transporter with damaged tail light was to be seen.

In a side street, off the Centre, in a dead end with an old continuance of detached houses, I drove past a vehicle whose form seemed to me extremely famously.

»I believe I have found him,« I reported Marc. »A white transporter and I believe even Bag and a broken tail light in the fender to have seen.«

Slowly I went back and then I saw him. »If you see how I have said it, because scratch, depressions and the broken indicator.«

»Well then lets us call the police. Should they continue the work.«

»Häh, fancy sometimes, the transporter is empty, then we have acted with lemons. I do not think that are so silly and drag the animals the whole day with himself. We will wait here and keep under surveillance them. Maybe have even today a date, or lead us to her hiding place.«

1.4 The refuge

Our observation was only from short duration, because suddenly two men attacked hectically from bushes out, ran to the transporter and drove off in a hurry.

In a sure distance we followed them, let overtake over and over again from a vehicle, so that constantly the same vehicle was not to be seen in the rear-view mirror and they could suppose thus the suspicion of the pursuit.

They drove out of the village, further on an unlit country road in the direction of north. Hardly vehicles were on the move here and thus we made our distance a little greater.

»Man, merely retains him in the eye,« I spoke to Marc. »In the glove compartment lie small binoculars, maybe you can better look with where he goes there.«

The journey went on, by smaller settlements which have more the idyll of a farm. A place where people like in the Middle Ages lived, worked with cattle, fields and dung and where some town children take vacation.

»You him turns there in front,« Marc interrupted my trains of thought. »Go more slowly, that has turned on the right on a country lane. Let us shortly before the way hold and see how far goes generally there in.«

We got out, crept to the country lane and in not too wide distance I see how the stoplights of the transporter signaled the clues. There something must be what made me curious. Thus I spoke:

» Pay attention rather and act in such a way, as if you must pee. I sneak up me by the thicket closer to see what is wrong there behind.«

»Should we not call rather the police, nevertheless, they are paid for such a shit application.«

»Yes, however, with which proofs you want to justify his application? So just mouth and go pee.«

I crept by the wood where a tree stands beside the other and one believes himself as if one stands in the wood. Since thousands of years they accompany the life of the people and her rushing works reassuringly on the characters. As a child we climbed with pleasure such trees up and this sway of the branches under the feet we felt as a special kick.

Further I marched warily by the undergrowth, stepped constantly in some holes in which my feet got caught and brought me to case. Then none fifty meters away a weak light. I approached step by step, with stagnant steps, pulled every time the air by my closed teeth if a branch broke under my feet.

In about ten meters of distance I stopped in the thicket and looked to the light that from a lamp came above the front door. It is an old dilapidated building, this identifies before the worldwide economic crisis better times had seen and now awaits his decay. Besides a barn with partly skew roof and missing disks in the windows.

Suddenly the front door rose, a man came out and went in the direction of scales. Immediately the motion dispatch rider switched on the lighting on the atrium and read them ablaze shine.

I winced, drew my head further and concentrated not to move, to give no sound of myself. The man opened the gate of this building used sometimes once for the agriculture and a mighty squeak and creak originated. Then I saw the transporter how he stood in the barn.

After a short moment the man appeared again, closed the gate, once more with creaky and squeaky sounds and disappeared again in the house. Minutes later the light also went out and it was dark again.

Startled I fell from the squat on the side when I felt a hand on my shoulder. Level in the undergrowth recumbent I looked up and hardly spoke audibly:

»Say sometimes you are goofy, I would have liked almost in faint. What you make here, nevertheless, you should pee there in front.«

»Ha, ha, stand you there in front sometimes and just "him" as long as in the wind, although no more drop out comes. What have you discovered up to now?«

»The transporter stands there in the barn, on the atrium a motion dispatch rider is right and the gate gives extremely loudly bruits of itself if one opens it.«

»And what you want to make now,« replied Marc.

»I will creep up from the side in the scales and try to see by the window something. Hopefully are not there still some motion dispatch riders. You keep an eye on the entrance as long as and if what acts itself, make an owl's bruit or is not able you also.«

»What does an owl make for bruits?« asked Marc.

»As well as we had always made as

children, oh forget it, pay attention rather that nobody comes.«

Step by step I groped the way in ducked position at the head, quite slowly I crept by the undergrowth and, nevertheless, it cannot be avoided stepping over and over again on dry branches which caused a cracking sound under the feet. Sighing I pulled through the air between the closed teeth, as if I wanted to suppress the bruits with it.

Then I stood on middle height of the building, darted over and looked by the window located on head height. However, a lot I could not recognize, only the transporter which obstructed a large part of the view. On tiptoe I went along the house wall to the next window, however, was also not to be seen there a lot. Thus I tried to rise by this open window, as behind me Marc whisper to me spoke:

»If I wait helps you.«

»Oh man, must frighten you me always so?«

Silently he crossed his hands on abdominal height, it positioned itself with down outstretched arms and slightly spread bones before me, so that I could use his hands as a degree.

A robber's leader, so we had called them children if we wanted to overcome some obstacles. Besides, we used the shoulder as an additional degree to overcome even higher distances.

With a jerk I was within the scope of this opening, while sometimes a cast-iron arched window was. It was extremely dark in this barn, nothing could see, not sometimes where I had jumped there. However, I had luck to trip over nothing. Thus I went for the moment to the transporter, opened the door and pleased me about this a little luck that stood on my side. The interior lighting was defective and the windows were equipped with mechanical technology. However, whether in addition still signal givers exist for certain functions, I could not recognize.

Thus I wound down the side disk, the door pushed shut almost silently again, reached by the open window and switched on the sidelight. Bright illuminated the space which was so big that umpteen tractors burst had, including tedder, spinning top mowers, baling press, liquid manure barrel as well as hay for a wide range of animals.

I went round the vehicle only junk saw on the one hand lying around, from humidity decayed wood and from the rust ruined steel, on the other side a grid shed. Three cats considered in it, sat squatted in the corner. In the weak light of the back floodlights I recognized Tommy.

»Eye Tommy, master is here,« I whispered and immediately he came, purred and can be fondled by my fingers which I stretched by the bars against him.

»Now dad gets out you here.« Nevertheless, the grid shed was bolted with a padlock.

»I get only one forceps, am there immediately again and then we go home.«

I looked for tools, for a forceps or in such a way, looked in the vehicle, however, could not recognize, because the rear side windows were sealed. Also the rear disks of the rear door admitted no insight and thus I opened them quietly. I got a fright when I in the interior cages found with the skin of the vehicle were connected, around them before involuntary ones slip to protect.

The cages were empty, however, at least twenty animals could accommodate at the same time. A measure animal theft, probably for any group the reliability of a product wants to test. They sit in her sound-isolated special rooms and try to check the inadequacy of a product with small animals. A test him is tested around the test security to test.

Here for this purpose such thieves like this receive the order to procure animals. Besides, it makes no difference to the groups, where from they come. With failure of such a test die it either or it leaves lifelong damages to the poor beings.

Quietly I closed the door with a moving again when just at the moment Marc murmured murmuring:

»Gerard, it somebody comes, hides.«

Shit I thought what make me now only. First I switched off the light, stood suddenly even in dark and did not know where. Now the window has to close no sense, would last too long.

I heard like the gate moved, was in considering where I should hide me, only one single possibility found without somewhere tripping noise to cause, to creep away me simply under the car. Here I lay in the mud and hoped that the type does not have the idea to leave now by the car.

Bright the light of the outside lighting seemed in the barn when the man went along the kerbside to the corner and beat off there a cap. A box with beer appeared. He took some bottles and stole them in a bag. Carefully he put back the cap again, took the bag and went in the direction of driver's side.

I closed the eyes and prayed to all divinities which spontaneously occurred to me that he did not note the open window. Sweat ran to me in brooks of the forehead, gathered in the orbits and caught in to burn. My heartbeat became quicker, the pulse higher and higher and my head threatened to burst.

All at once he stopped and exactly in my eye level. He put the bag on the ground, beside his to long trousers which the shoes infiltrated by the dirt covered. Then I heard like myself the carriage door opened, he swung himself in on which the carriage went about some centimeters to the knees.

Here stuck I lay, now could not move any more, saw only the subsoil muddy by dirt.

My thoughts ran there that he will immediately leave and sees lying me in the floodlight before his carriage, however, then I noted the bag on the ground. I laid my head at the side to the right to be able to catch other bruits better with the ear. A crack was to be heard and afterwards a clong, as if the glove compartment was opened and was closed again.

He got out again and sore metallic scratching was to be heard when the vehicle fell back in his ergonomic basic position. I moved quite carefully further to the right, so that he did not note me while bending down to his bag, however, suddenly I hung with my pullover on a bell of the exhaust firmly.

Shit I thought. My heart caught in wildly and loudly to knock, so loud that it could hear fictitiously seen in the vicinity from twenty meters everybody.

The man wound the side window high, bent down a little, felt with a hand for the bag, raised him and as a result disappeared from the barn. Squeaky bruits were still to be heard when the gate was closed.

By a narrow gap of the door I saw that the light had not went out yet and thus I waited that, finally, it goes out. There passed seconds, seconds to one seemed like minutes, extremely long minutes. Then it was getting dark and I was able to stir. By force I tore the pullover of the bell, so that a bruit originated, as if all teeth from the titan's lamellas of a zipper burst. Then I moved under the vehicle and crept to the window.

With both hands I held on in the masonry, pushed off with the feet from the ground to land with the knees in the aperture. Besides, I tore open to me the trousers. Responsible, I imagined, why I also draw for such actions material trousers and not jeans which are a lot of robust.

I squeezed my upper part of the body by the aperture and dropped myself forward out. Besides, I chafed to me the hand bales and because my things were already broken everywhere, it made no difference to me to wipe the mud of the hands in the pullover.

Quick I disappeared in the thicket and immediately Marc met me and asked what I would have found.

»It was very dark there in it, this is why I have turned on the light of the transporter. In the transporter itself have been only cages, but no animals in it. Behind in the corner a grid box stands in three cats are locked up, among the rest, also Tommy. However, the box is closed and thus I had looked for tools, indeed, had found nothing, and would have also been too nice. Then there came one boy and got beer, there I had hidden under the carriage, until he disappeared again. I hope that itself so much thought does not make around the open carriage window what he had too wound again. If discuss for the moment for hours it who had left open the window, they will fast note that somebody was there. Man you, I has sweated glanders and water there under the carriage.«

»This I can fancy, but now, nevertheless, with the proofs we can call the police. By the way, what you have made with your things, looks like a tramp.«

»Shit on the things! What does the police use to us? For a search warrant our proofs are not sufficient which no proofs are again because we have nothing concrete in the hand. Now we go for the moment home, get a bolt tailor and then we come back again.«

Dirtily I looked, as if I had worked three layers one after the other unterdays in the coal mining, however what one does not do everything for his cat.

1.5 The redemption

At home I changed fast, then ran in the cellar and looked for the bolt tailor, nevertheless, did not find him. My consideration was valid whom I had lent him. Mostly these are the neighbors who steal borrowed objects without a trace or destroy by improper treatment.

»Marc, have I lent you sometimes my bolt tailor?«

»Yes, but this dates back for a long time, at that time I had used him for my mesh fence. But you have got back him shortly after again because I had bought to myself one.«

»I do not know where I mean there has lost. Do you have yours in handy suture?

»Lies with me in the cellar.«

»Then is deprived to us him.«

We briefly drove past with Marc. While Marc looked in his cellar for the bolt tailor, Denise about our intentions grilled me:

»Person makes only no shit if to you get to touch, they know certainly no fun. Maybe they are even armed and shoot possibly still at you or torment you.«

»What would you make if your cats

disappear and you know where they are?«

Rest entered, she knew no answer, wanted to say no answer and, nevertheless, I knew, she would just react, incite her man to such action.

When Marc came again from the cellar and brought, in addition, another two flashlights, got on the way to us. Clouds gathered all of a sudden and it caught just now in to rain. Rain is always tiresome, mostly one is never properly drawn, as well as today. Slowly we also heard rumbling the clouds and as from mind hand originated strange flickering light, as if somebody the creepy weather takes photos became. On the other hand it is good to know that the rain falls on everybody, on the arms and the empires, on the young and on the old people, on person and also on animal.

Everywhere black clouds were to be seen which were torn like a reservoir by the flash and thunder and the rains flood-like to ground dropped. Trace grooves provided for exponential piling up of meter-high waves and gave to the windshield wipers no chance to fight against it. The country road was empty to recognize no back lights of advance-moving vehicles which could show the way. Thus we approached just at a speed which hardly differs from the maximum speed of a land tortoise our aim.

After fairly long time we reached the country lane and briefly behind it I half stopped on the side stripe, switched off the light and drew off the key. Then I waited, hoped that the rain would immediately decrease. Like drum beats the raindrops drummed on the roof of the vehicle and everywhere puddles formed.

»If no sense has to sit around here, the thing lets us behind us bring. As well as it looks, the rain will still continue hours. Moreover, can it only be an advantage, because who goes out into the streets already in the weather?«

Armed with flashlight, bolt tailor and transport basket, we crept by the wet undergrowth of this woodland. Everywhere grew to jaws, a tree itself to the wind and the light gives away and of that not always grew just is, so that many crowns got caught into each other. The rain so intensely on us could not thereby fall down. Still I felt after a while, like wet my trouser legs, shoes and also socks were.

Slowly we approached the house. It was somber, up to the lamp in the input area, and in his light one sees like the rain thick strings sidelong to ground trickles leaves.

We crept by the thicket, to the scale side, as sudden a dog started to bark.

Stunningly we stopped in squat, looked around and there I saw a sheepdog running around the house which was bound in a chain which passed just spot up to the entrance.

»Where comes then all at once. Nevertheless, he was not there just now yet. The poor animal must sleep with rain outdoors.«

The dog barked further and woke up the men. Light began in the house and seconds later a man stepped before the house and shouted:

»Rex! Shut up you make silly cur, that you on your place comes, but smartly!«

With the forefinger around the house showing the man stood before the dog. Nevertheless, he further barked, made the man furious on which he took a floor and shut to the animal. With drawn tail the dog ran around the corner and avoided thus our field of vision. Howling tones were to be heard how one cry or whimper.

Then the guy with the dog in the neckband came leading around the corner, went to the shed and enclosed him there. I was to be rushed near, besides, at the guy who ill-treated the dog, however, Marc held back me and spoke in the mild sound to me:

»This has no sense, you do not know where the other is, or how many these are generally. Maybe the dog still feels threatened and attacks still you.«

»You are right, we may rush nothing, but how I come now in the scales, without the dog tears to pieces me.«

»Here maybe we should break off and try to the police knows close with what is traded here.«

»I replied one, I have gone so far,« I replied Marc. »Now I also want to pull through it.«

»Yes, but how?«

»I must try to win the trust of the dog. If his rules of etiquette were spoken constantly in the imperious armed forces jargon, he is maybe receptive to a few affectionate words.«

»Nevertheless, you do not want to get in possibly there, fondle possibly still the dog. Ah, I already see, you want! Then get I already bandage stuff.«

»Oh just, nevertheless, the valve, to me already passes nothing. Pay attention you here rather!«

Extremely slowly I rose, shouted in extremely give way, reassuring and trust-waking sound positions the name of the dog:

»Reeex, Rexi, Rex my smaller more sweetly, where is then my Rex.«

One I seemed to me, as if I talked to an edentate one whose mouth is still booked with a teat. Slowly I moved forward, over and over again the names of the dog calling. Then I saw him in the windowless breakthrough on I shut. Only half a head with the pricked up ears and the far torn open eyes was to be seen.

Further I shut to him, talked with him in an extremely quiet sound about the weather, about the bad boys and about Tommy who is held prisoner behind him in the shed.

When I had reached the building, we saw ourselves for some seconds in the eyes and I still spoke further, of the Bad and good, of bad and beauty in this world. Carefully he listened, concentrated his look at me and thus I let a little bit halting my hand walk by the opening which was sniffed first by him and can be stroked then by her.

I had a few more little leakage rakes in the trouser pocket which I had taken for Tommy. However, now Rex should have some of it, around maybe still a little bit more trust to me to develop. For a full-grown sheepdog the pair of things were something for him get tooth, still I noticed that he accepted the pair of crisp pockets with thanks.

Marc came over and made our robber's leaders again, so that I better came by the orifice. Beaming with delight the dog received me, waved hectically his tail to and fro and can be stroked extensively. Crouching I sat beside him, further talked about the things of the everyday need, while he leant against me and my hand started to lick off with his tongue.

After a while I heard die to whispering words of Marc: »Make, finally, faster, we have to leave here.«

I laid the flashlight so to ground that it shone there to the grid box and then let me the bolt tailor reach by window. While a hand stroked the dog, I tried to break open with the other hand the castle. However, with a hand it was too complicated, I laid a few more little leakage rakes on the ground to occupy the dog and while all three cats lay hissing in the extreme corner squatted, and I cracked the castle.

Quick I crept in, Tommy reached to me and when I wanted out, Rex stood leant on his rear paws against the door. Tommy put on his ears, deeper crept in my crook of the arm and caught dreadfully in to hiss and to growl.

»If is well Tommy, this is a friend who helps to us to come here out. He does nothing to you.« At the same time I spoke again in a leisurely voice with the dog:

»You are a fine dog, quite rather, now you must position yourself under it, so that I can open the door.«

Besides, I fondled him by the grid in the neck and after a while he let down himself, so that I could leave the cage. Unfortunately, I must leave behind both other cats, because I do not know to whom they belong, but for it the police will already provide, because now I have proofs enough, it has seen with own eyes.

I passed Tommy by the aperture, Marc took him and stowed away him in the cat's box. Then I braced myself high and jumped me outward. The dog stood there again in such a way that ears and eyes were to be seen. His look seemed to look sad what committed a crime almost the heart to me, however, I could not take him. If I did it, I would only identify with these criminals. However, now I had to contrive what that he does not resume to bark, before we are except reach.

With the decision that Tommy receives only his little leakage rakes at home I took the remaining and threw for the moment one by the aperture.

»Look,« I quietly spoke. »Search the fine little leakage rake, look.«

Immediately he turned round, looked and after not even one second he stood there again. I threw a second, then two all at once and too last the rest.

While the dog looked for the crisp pillow, I ran in the wood. Marc was quite wide ahead, at least I did not see him. It still rained, indeed, not more so really, had accustomed me in the meantime also to cold wet that my things sopped. Dragging I walked through the shrubbery, had to think of both cats and the dog. Will the cats find again her owners whom dog receive a new home?

However, all at once I felt beside myself what run. I completely got a fright, had counted on wild animals like wild boars and other, but not with it. Beaming with delight with waving tail, Rex jumped at me and tore me to ground.

»If is well my sweet, is a dear dog. But I cannot take you, then I would just be a criminal, how your current owners. Decrease again, I will provide for the fact that you get a better home.«

He did not give up me, accompanied me

further although I over and over again tried to send back him. Then I saw like Marc hectically on myself it came up whom upwards pointing outstretched forefinger spoke over and over again on the mouth beating and whispering to me:

»Pssssst, the bulls stand there in front and look to themselves at your car.«

»Deal nothing else, than to have a look at parking vehicle.«

»Probably not. What is with the dog?«

»He must have jumped by the window and now runs to me behind. To bring back him would not be useful a lot, possibly he would run again behind me. If I bind him, we must calculate on the fact that he starts to bark and then the guys in the arse have. He must stay here and I hope that he decreases again in the scales.«

Slowly and gently we crept in the direction of country road, saw the police vehicle directly standing before my car. Shit, I thought what they make there bare. If one needs them sometimes really, they never are there.

Finally, after fairly long time they went on and thus we bumped to the car, swung us and disappeared with a gentleman's start which tore deep grooves in the wet ground of the roadway limitation.

I left behind the dog and in the rear-view mirror I see him still for a short time how he sat in the street edge, then he disappeared in the wood. Thoughts spread to my head, thoughts as probably his future destiny will look.

»Where is the bolt tailor?« Marc interrupted my thoughts.

»I have forgotten shit, that there, just the flashlight. I buy to you a new one and a new flashlight you should also have. Had you looked sometimes at the street sign, how is the way called?«

 »Yes, this is the country lane number fifty-five.«

»Fifty-five, OK. Thanks!«

When I went past to a telephone box, I stopped.

»What do you want here?« I was asked.

»The bull's call, before the crooks notice that was broken and a cat is absent.«

I chose the emergency phone number of the police and reported:

»If they go in the country lane fifty-five purely, a little bit ruined farm in which at least two men live stands about in hundred meters of distance. Beside the house is a barn in which domestic animals are held prisoner to resell them possibly in experiment institutions. At the moment only two cats exist, as well as a dog who is ill-treated by the owner.

If they more exactly look the transporter, they will see that it concerns here professional thieves. I would not like to mention my names to them for safety reasons, please they understand this.«

I hung up and went on, further home. Tommy miaowed incessantly and it sounded like this miaow to the satisfaction. Satisfaction also climbed up in me to have Tommy again with me, finally, it is my job to provide for the fact that it goes well to him.

1.6 An anonymous expression of thanks

It was already wide after midday night when I with Marc still in my cellar bar transferred around our successful mission to water with a beer. Long we still talked about the disappearance of domestic animals, hope that it appears after few days again; the searches in the neighborhood, at animal homes; this switch from indications and the suspension of pamphlets.

If all that does not lead to a result, only the information helps to the police, for the purpose of the registration, where, when and how often the suspicion on an animal theft was expressed. However, in most cases, even policemen cannot help.

The next day ran again normally, in the morning Tommy stood in the terrace door and wanted out, only the annoyance flowed through my body over and over again if I saw like he walked there.

With a specific sentence he scaled the partition wall of the neighbor, disappeared behind it to get himself his early morning meals with the close bipeds. Afterwards the visit of his congeners, the ostentatious reporting about the last cruel hours in to a dungeon and the splendid and miraculous occurrence with gangsters, bandits, criminals and delinquent. Maybe he must fetch to himself also for the moment the absolution at his cat's lady, for the unpredictable absenteeism of a thrilling date. Who knows what in such small brains goes forward.

However, how usual he also was now again about midday, early afternoon at home, brought now and then sometimes one of his friends, either with the thick grey fur or with the paintbrushes in the ears, every now and then also sometimes to me absolutely unknown one.

It is an animal friendship and one does not know, however whether it is considered purpose-engaged, behavior of utilization or friendly. Friendship is a virtue which is similar very much that of the people.

Today is one day where letter boxes are overcrowded with advertisement and daily papers which are financed by the advertising-propelling economy. A favorable variation to find out about local news. Today particularly an article with the heading struck me: *Anonymous phone call smashes animal catcher's ring.*

Then the report of an unknown caller who gave the instruction to a hiding place where possibly itself audacious animal catchers considered the domestic animals from the neighboring places caught to appropriate financial profits then by the sales to test institutions.

In addition, a bolt tailor was found with whom the castle of the shed was broken open in which another two cats were. Further one more flashlight whose allocation is still uncertain was found. Two men resident there were accused of the animal theft and were taken into custody.

The police suppose that more than only two cats has been in the cage would have to go, because, otherwise, no reason would exist to break open the castle. This was also protested by the delinquents.

There was possible manner even more culprits where it came to a quarrel of all partners who separated as a result and had fetched now a part of her prey.

Nevertheless, from a sheepdog whom the anonymous caller mentioned any trace is missing.

I called immediately Marc to draw the attention of him to this article:

»Letterbox already emptied? Then go and get the daily paper. On the page two a very interesting report on animal theft. It seems to me very much famously what is written there thus. Your bolt tailor they have also found, can fetch him on the guard.«

»Ha, ha, ha. I can take the piss out of myself alone, I have already read it. Fancy sometimes, they get out who has been this. Burglary, theft, trespass, material damage, kidnapping and I do not know still what everything. This becomes quite a nicely long record.

Yesterday my opponent asked me whether he could borrow the bolt tailor sometimes because his screed mats must be reduced. I could not give to him because I had nobody more. Today he told me in a ridiculous form that my bolt tailor lay in the exhibit room of the police. Very wittily I do not find this!«

»This has not meant, nevertheless, thus. Where from he should also know this, nevertheless, you say yourself that he, besides has laughed. He has read it with the bolt tailor in the newspaper and makes only one fun from it to himself! Yes and a thousand times Excuse me, I have not come yet to buy to you a new one. Tomorrow I will go to the property market and buy to myself also immediately one.«

»This is not so important, you need to me no new one shop, I am able to do this also alone. But I do not get the feeling off that everybody points with the finger at me.

Sometimes look me so peculiarly.«

»Who should have got there already what? If we shut up, nobody will notice what, moreover, I have fetched back to me only my property. Finally, is Tommy MY cat and in an experiment institution MY cat has to search nothing. No animal has there what search, not sometimes the sheepdog.«

It is the bad conscience what tormented us not to close the art the eyes for the dirty work which one has done and develops the feelings negative now because one believes to have acted some wrong. It is the scruple which plays a role in the faith, in the philosophy, the ethics, the art and the right.

After ending of the conversation I thought about the dog. What planned with him, he should be also passed to the testing above the table? The poor guy where he has only remained has hopefully found he a new home.

Precisely at this moment Tommy ran past just me and I felt joy, joy that he is there again. In times of the loneliness, Tommy was there always for me and in times of the recollection he sat beside me and divided them with me.

The next day I met my neighbor on the street, the chatterbox of our village; a blabbermouth between real virtuality and virtual reality. She gets to drivel to one a rissole to the ear without owning the decency, offering mustard with:

»I have belonged that Tommy had disappeared and that he is there again. However, this is nice. The culprits have caught them red-handed. These were right professionals, with those was not to be joked … and the cats, were found also are again with her masters. One was the cat of Mrs. Susebier, nevertheless, they know, the older lady with the grey curtains before the window which always with the mailman a little liqueur drinks. She has been glad as the police them brought …, and Tommy …, was brought also by the police?«

I nodded only because I no desire had to me the day with a long and irritating conversation free of sense to verse meadows.

»Then, nevertheless, the police has been right with her supposition.«

Supposition? Curiosity packed me all at once what she meant with supposition. Does know them possibly more than I believe to know? Though well her son-in-law works at the police, but he is responsible more or less only for writing down of parking ticket. Moreover, he visits once in a blue moon his mother-in-law, but as the chance wants in such a way, nevertheless, maybe he has chatted a little bit from the school bag what he is allowed to do not really.

»How do they get on?« I asked.

»Well, nevertheless, the police believed that more cats were held prisoner. Two had found them and now with Tommy these would already be three.«

Shit I thought, within the next half an hour, know the whole village about this entertainment. If something must contrive to me again, some lies. Oh I hate such situations in which one is pursued by such events.

»Is sorry me, I do not know what they mean. Tommy was never away, but we can talk another spot about it, now I have to go. Wishes to them still a nice day.«

I disappeared and on the way I let pass everything once more revue. Does start now like Miss Marple bridging her boredom by new occupation fields as a keen amateur detective? Or is it to be had to know her curiosity everything, the search for the ultimate kick?

Already in the book "Struwwelpeter" sent a reminder the history of little Pauline with the lighter that it will come to a sad end if one plays curiously with matches.

The next day when I came at noon from the work home, I tripped almost over a present that stood before the door. A present muffled in colored paper without senders, but with a map of the following text:

Who has the courage,
to exert itself for a fair thing,
is able for himself and others
a lot move.
Thanks!

I was dismayed a little about this expression of thanks, associated this moral obligation with the theft of the cats, nevertheless, asked myself at the same time who would lie behind. First I had my neighbor, the chatterbox in suspicion, but she would look rather with her daughter for a present with which she can act then so as if it was to her "Even bought". Then I thought of Mrs. Susebier who thinks, actually, very practically and gives away shower gels because it owns the odor of the wide world, almost like an expensive perfume.

When I opened the present, the reasonable suspicion was kept me against Mrs. Susebier unsuccessfully.

A bottle the noblest cognac appeared, a brandy from the region cognac in the

Department Charente in France. In addition two hand-polished glasses, with a short handle and wide belly which becomes rejuvenated upwards there. A glass for swinging of the noble drink and for unfolding of the bouquet.

While I read the label of the flask, the phone rang. I accepted the conversation and immediately Marc babbled off:

»I come unsuspectingly home, Denise was still with her sport when I found a bag with two packages before the door. First I thought of a mistake, however, there a name was nowhere to be found and thus I took them with purely. Inside I have unpacked them then and ...«

»Let me advice,« I interrupted him. »There a flask of cognac, two glasses and an expression of thanks was in it. Is right or am I right?«

»Where from do you know this, is it of you? Have I forgotten something? I already, nevertheless, had birthday, you know this.«

»No no, no thought makes to you around, I have received the same one. It is a sort of expression of thanks of an anonymous donator, probably for the announcement which we have made.«

»But who can this have been?«

»No notion, it should also not hang largely on bell. We take it as well as it is and fungus about that.«

I pour out myself a cognac, sat down on the terrace and observed Tommy how he was just running behind on two bones to a butterfly that was by a height inaccessible for him. I thought just of the strain he gave to me when I searched him; to the unusual feeling to miss him. And just at the moment where he was not on my side my heart showed only much too clearly that it has become for a long time a part of my life. A road companion who goes along together the street with me and does not turn away if a crossroad appears.

It was a meeting for life when we saw ourselves the first time, recognizing a close soul which will accompany us for years.

Completely of consumption I swung the glass in the circle, my nose held in the edge and inhaled the bouquet of this brandy stored in oaken barrels deeply. Then he flowed gulp, softy, softly about the tongue and brought all taste nerves to the efflorescence.

1.7 Another occupant

Tommy was further occupied to catch the butterfly who refreshed himself in the meantime in the extensive nectar spring of the upright standing, thick, grape-like, dark-violet blossoms of the lilac.

In ducked position, with whipping tail and a timorous look he crouches before it and observed the butterfly whose drawings on the wings look like dangerous animal eyes. They serve as a camouflage before the various predators and should warn by her remarkable staining about her danger.

With shaky lower jaw he let tones sound which strongly remind of the rattles of teeth. These are not he no animals may, it is only that certain untouchable hierarchy must be considered and of which a butterfly will never get hold an absolutely aiming and luxurious rank, as long as Tommy is the boss of this property.

Quick he gave up again him when this rose in the winds and fluttered of it. As a result he lay down in the middle of the ground cover directly on the yellow blossoms, caught in to yawn and closed bit by bit his eyes.

If now I got up, he would wake up all of a sudden and run behind me, because of fear, he could miss what. Or if one rings now in the door, he would be already in the door before I me generally would have raised, as if he expected visit.

If it is not then a visitor he knows, he runs like an offended liverwurst by the flat. If it is, however, somebody he knows and may, then he sits down before it and observes favorably the communication with the guest.

The evening demonstrated the day slowly in Deep-blue to black and thus I withdrew to follow my essential night employment, to sleeping.

The next morning I got up relatively early, went on the terrace and observed the glowing stripe in the horizon which made the light of the sun slowly visible.

Clouds were watch hardly and only slowly walked the upper edge of the glowing ball towards the horizon. A sight like the explosive process which emptied a fire-vomiting volcano. Sometimes I would leave the time and stay with an especially nice motive like today, a long time.

However, thus nicely a sunrise may be which allows beginning a new day, with him the work and with it also my employer also shouts.

When I came early in the afternoon home, I received nearly one psychic shock, almost like a fright rigidity which left me with open mouth, without moving in the car on the entrance.

On the stair to my entrance there lay a dog, a sheepdog. Medium-sized, hard with normal stature. His yellowish-brown fur with black badges in head and back, was unmistakable. It was Rex, I recognized him immediately and, actually, I was glad internally to see again him.

Halting I opened the carriage door and put outside a bone. Rex pricked up his ears, besides, tormented itself high and when I completely rose from the carriage, the gigantic animal jumped at me, tore me almost to ground and luck off my face.

»Eye Rex,« I spoke beaming with delight to him. »Where do you come then? Have you made the whole way alone or has somebody brought you? Walk in for the moment, you are hungry certainly.«

Immediately he looked himself into Tom's micron feeding bowls when we entered the kitchen. Like grannies the goat Bertha who had eaten the clothesline with socks, bedclothes and nappies blank Rex was about to lick out the feeding bowls of Tommy ready with cupboard.

I took a deep plate and filled some bowls of Tommy wet feed. Then I observed him how he devoured in a hurry the feed as he soaked up afterwards still the small Brekkies pallets with the avarice of a vacuum cleaner and decontaminated expertly in his abdomen.

Suddenly one rang in the door, I opened and Marc stood before it.

»Walk in, I have a surprise for you,« I spoke to him.

We went to the kitchen where Rex was about just with his tongue to clean the plates up to the last crumb.

»If I may introduce Marc, this is Rex, Rex this is Marc.«

»Rex? Nevertheless, this is not possibly …,« a short break entered and one noticed like he in consider was, before he further spoke: »…, nevertheless, not possibly Rex?«

»It seems in such a way, do not ask me like he has come. When I came home, he already lay before the door and waited.«

»Now,« said Marc, »dogs are able to do half a million spots better smelling, how the people. Thus they can pick up the scent who will remain forever concealed for us. The dog nose can perceive even the finest odor nuances and make a distinction of each other. And even under the most difficult conditions. Still after days they can still pursue the track of a person over hundreds of kilometers. Think only of the feel dogs, of guide dogs, to rescue dogs, to accompanying dogs and warning dogs.«

»Is right, you are right. There was sometimes a history where a dog has run four hundred kilometers away home because he had longing,« I interrupted Marc's implementation.

»Yes and in the traffic news one also hears over and over again from free running dogs. Exactly like the dog that was flung with a traffic accident on the highway from the car his owner seriously injured to the hospital came and afterwards he ran the highway up and down to find his master. For days the car station police and the protection of animals tried to catch the dog, however, in vain, until the seriously injured owner came together with an orderly and got him.«

»You mean him has found only the whole way here?«

»What you think then. It was probably the only one which had spoken sometimes nice words to him; he stroked with a meek kindhearted hand; he spread out his arms and embraced him who had an affectionate smile on the lips which was called welcome. Yes I believe you have found there a loyal friend who will never again leave you.«

»You mean, I should keep him?«

»Now Gerard, he is without man, why or do not see somewhere a dog brand in the neckband?«

»How I should tell only Tommy.«

And not to expect how differently, just Tommy came unsuspectingly around the corner and welcomed Rex with terrible hissing. Immediately he rebelled, looked by the hump equally substantially bigger and signaled thus his attack readiness and he remained with all four on the ground to take the flight if necessary fast.

Again horrific hissing and the hump which left him bigger and more immense appeared, as if he itself with this gymnastic exercise on a forthcoming sports event prepares would become. The tail was thick like a stove flue, the bones stiffly like the locomotion on stilettos and the lateral duct strongly reminded of the behavior pattern of a pouch cancer.

With the courage, as if he swam sinking ships against and the bravery to Neanderthal men with elastic clubs the heads to hit he approached the dog. It is, as if one with a roast chicken with the veterinarian turns up to enquire whether still what is to be made.

He raised his paw, showed his extremely sharp claws and moved his facial play into a fear-giving killer look. However, Rex was interested a little in the belligerence of Tommy, stood beside me and looked at the cat with slightly inclined head.

»Tooooommmmy, this leaves, this is Rex and Rex here the next time will probably have to live. He is our friend …, and therefore also your friend!«

Tommy kept quiet, sat down, however, and did not let out of sight the dog. Whipping his tail hit to and fro, a warning signal for the opponent. The cat was ready to strike immediately, to defend his empire and also his autocracy. Courage and bravery are the guarantors for the knightly virtue.

»Rex, this is Tommy. Tommy is our cat and friend. He is after the hierarchy of the rank order the boss here in the house.«

Rex made seat, directed the ears forwards, allowed to hatchel the mouth open and the tongue hang out. Then light one whimper, a happy one whine, wanted to go to Tommy, pass to him the hand to the friendship, however, I held on him to the neckband. Then I lured Tommy who came up as a result quite without any hurry to me and his ovally narrowed eyes did not leave from Rex. A signal for his belligerence.

I asked Marc the dog to stick and while I stroked with a hand Tommy, the other hand stroked his back over Rex. Well noticeably both liked it. As a result Rex lay down on the side, with the back to Tommy and gave with it a trustworthy gesture of himself.

For the first time I let Rex on the roofed terrace sleep, a kennel built to him with intimated windows and a half-open roofed porch with window boxes and flowerpots.

It lasted some days, until the both had got used each other. For this purpose I took the first day-offs to let feel to my both sutures, in this however, thus unusual situation.

With a towel I had rubbed off Rex hard the fur and had laid this beside Tom's micron bed, so that he had got used to the smell of the dog. In the beginning Tommy found the dog smell only "Bah", however, ever on occasion he smelt in it, the more he got used to it.

I did the same one with Tommy and laid it beside Rex of his cap. Immediately he pushed his snout deeply in the cloth, inhaled the odoriferous substances so, as if he prepared as a feel dog for the search for explosives.

While Tommy carried out in the morning his walk in the neighborhood, I got Rex in the flat, with it I calms to work could go.

After some days, Rex lay in the residential room at the side on his cover and looked out to the terrace door when Tommy walked just in. Slowly the cat shut to Rex and sniffed in detail in him. Then he also lay down at the side before him and both looked. The ice seemed to have broken at this moment, still I did not trust the peace up to the nasal point and let during the day Rex furthermore stay in the flat, while Tommy ran in the neighborhood.

It is like the story of the Aesop where the lion positioned himself ill and he asked all animals to his sickbed in his pit. Only the clever fox hesitated to enter the pit. The fox answered a suitable question of the lion there: »I would already enter into your pit if I did not see that so many tracks led out in, but none.«

1.8 The summons

When I came on the next day home and emptied the mailbox, I found two letters of the police. A little bit surprised, I turned the letters to and fro, she looked to me from all sides and thought about it in which radar case I have gone that to me to immediately two penalty notices are sent.

However, first I went for a walk with Rex. He loves these extensive walks to pee on his family tree, to rave above meadows and fields and retrieving the floor thrown by his master. Also on the small visit of the mailman or a meddlesome insurance agent he can jump, he is grateful every time. Besides, jumping is not meant nastily, he would only like to play just.

While Rex was occupied I thought of the radar traps which took two artistic photos of me in Black and white and which were sent me now with a shocking calculation in the house. Nowadays extremely modern devices are in use an application, with a sophisticated photography method which can spot of every pimple of a pubescent acne sick person. The photos are so pin sharp that one could use them with a suspension of the driving license, immediately for the new one.

Both images I will deeply engrave in the

brain and in future probably a little more slowly must go, because two photos on one day reach, quite actually.

The behavior of such radar devices is able to do with a psychic grandpa's table groundhog will compare who is lying in wait without moving for days, around then with a sneaking up dwarf's Peringuey's Adder to identify a little bit raised speed. Radar devices use, on this occasion, an underhand weapon: an incredibly irritating flash; groundhogs, however, her brain, because they know how toxic a dwarf's Peringuey's Adder can be.

Coming at home again, I took both letters to the hand around them to open when Tommy with a short "Groan, Groaning" showed as a result that his feeding bowls must be still filled.

»Oh excuse Tommy, I has not forgotten you! I had sunk only into thoughts where I could have flashed.«

After I had fed all animals, I went to the sitting room to open, finally, my post. The first one was a writing of the ordinal velvet with a warning for a ridiculous action:

They parked inadmissibly on one
very used country road,
in a blind curve
and thereby hindered him

the following traffic.

Wow, I thought, a very used street with a blind curve where was it then? With the country road one could have seen in both directions the horizon if the weather does not shit so would have been. Then still the tip:

The warning becomes only effective,
if they agree with it
and the exemplary fine
within one week pay.

All right? A consent is like Erlangen of a permission; how the approval that my washing machine suppresses constantly a sock; like the approval to turn a tree to make loo paper from it; to take like the authorization, as a taxi driver money if people are carried.

My car stood at the wrong time at a wrong place and now became the regimentation of the Highway Code. I opened the second letter and got a fright. These were summons as a witness in the preliminary proceedings because of suspicion of the theft, with threat of penalty payment and presentation in handcuffs with nonappearance.

»Really,« I imagined, »how come only on me?«

One week later I was on the guard to this conversation what ran on various questions, why, why and which is why my vehicle stood just at a place where shortly after a police application had taken place and in which respect I stood to the suspects.

The difference between a conversation and a questioning primarily consists in the fact that it no friend is with one talks, but a policeman who put questions over and over again. A high-level complex underpinned what needs costly methods and technologies on which the policeman meant:

»Examinations, questionings or also witness's statements serve to find to the truth as well as also the decision-making. Their statement, they had gone for peeing deeper to the wood, then had positioned themselves because of the rain under a row of densely standing together trees under, we cannot understand. We have to a case are given with which it is about animal theft. Indeed, the suspicion of the likelihood is supposed here increasingly that other cats were stolen by self-justice.«

»A supposition which were expressed by the suspects« I interrupted the flow of words of the law guardian. »Nevertheless, yes, however, this is in order if somebody fetches back his property again, nevertheless, this is pure self-help.«

»From self-help any more the speech cannot be here, because the appropriation stands in connection with a burglary. This burglary puts a criminal offence continuance with striking characters of the theft where an animal was stolen in the intention to appropriate it illegal.«

»Nevertheless, one can appropriate no property illegal if one is already an owner. However, we go out sometimes from it, somebody has got his cats really again. How, otherwise, the cat would have come to her owner. Do they mean, she runs by itself again home? It was often enough discussed enough how policemen behave if the theft of a domestic animal is indicated. Smiled became such indications and thus I can understand every animal holder if he reaches to own jurisdiction, as long as no physical damage originates.«

It was quiet all at once to say nobody been capable something. Besides, my uniformed interlocutor was to be come along notes, a sort of protocol about these negotiations. However, then I interrupted the rest to deflect him of some negative thoughts:

»Some years ago a donkey was prosecuted in Egypt for the theft of a corncob with an imprisonment of one day and his holder with a fine. Here I ask myself, how petty must the person still become if one calls the police because of theft of one single corncob? Besides, it was not sometimes theft, but oral space, because while the person commits a theft with the hand, the donkey has robbed in the truest sense of the word with the mouth.«

»We speak here not of donkeys and corncobs, but of a criminal offence which refers to animal theft,« spoke the policeman energetically to me.

»I understand what they mean,« I replied to him. »You try to filter out here from a criminal offence another criminal offence. It is one for lack of zebras as if, simply provides a few donkeys with the suitable stripes.«

Our conversation which existed of scrap of unclear circumstances ran quite unilaterally. Not to reveal me as a culprit, I tried to answer a question with a counter question over and over again.

After one-hour questioning I might leave the guard again, with the tip that the public prosecutor's office would further look after the case. I should think over my statement again, because one would carry out if necessary a comparison with the fingerprints in the bolt tailor and mine.

Shit I thought came as me home. What

should become only from the dog and the cat if I sit in the jail. I called Marc and asked him on a little beer to go past. Then I told about the uncomfortable questioning, from which why, why, which is why by which.

»And what you have said on it,« asked me Marc.

»I have said that I was peeing in the wood and when it started to rain So really, me under the close together standing trees subordinated, until it became less.«

»Delightfully, what better a lot we probably not one.«

»Yes what should I tell him then, otherwise that I have pinched my own cat? He has scooped however, thus and thus already suspicion.«

»Pee, on the country road, in the middle of the wood, with rain, this I would also not feel as plausible.«

»Tomorrow I will go to the lawyer and consult. Fancy sometimes, I have to go in jail. Does what make I with Tommy and Rex?«

»Come along no head therefore. If it had to go really thus his what I do not believe, however, then I take the animals so long to myself, nevertheless, this is clear!«

I made an appointment with a lawyer for the day after next, reports him the situation in which I was and asked around, his advice:

»This is already a daring thing. On the one hand it is quite understandable for me, my daughter also has a cat and loves them madly, but on the other hand she also shows a juridical criminal offence. Though the delinquents themselves have refunded no indication, have pointed out the police, nevertheless, to the fact that they had stolen more than only two cats. Moreover, the broken open castle and the bolt tailor was found what let's suppose another criminal offence which is followed up now by the ordinal authority.«

»Shit …, and what me I now?«

»It will probably run out to a judicial examination. For the time being we should revoke her statement and demonstrate the exact circumstances. In addition I will request for the moment for the inquiry act. Then we see what happen.«

I went home and immediately Rex jumped at me. A warm-humid respiration smelling of rumen intensely went to me in the nose and before I could escape, I already had the pink-colored gigantic washcloth in the middle of the face.

»Yes Rex, you are a fine dog. I also, nevertheless, please me.«

After he had got his strokes he gave up me. I sat down on the sofa and thought. Rex went outward, lay down on the lawn and observed the birds who fly past in the sky.

Tommy walked in, saw me sitting thoughtfully and jumped on sofa. He sat down beside me and waved about with a paw before my face, as if he tried the bladder of thought me coated to bring with the claws of his paw for bursting; to get out me of the state of the spiritual absence, to bring me, to follow the thread again strictly

»Oh Tommy, dad has shits made.«

Tommy lay down in the hollow of my femurs and caught loudly in to purr. Besides, I sank over and over again softly my hand about his fur.

»Actually, I have made no shit,« I further continued. »At least I would do it over and over again if somebody has the idea to kidnap you or to steal. So, however, dad probably has to go now in the prison, but Marc will pay attention as long as to them.«

Tommy turned round, laid his head a little at an angle, and looked at me, as if he had understood every word and assistance tried to perform with his presence. Then he positioned himself upright and prodded with the put aside head over and over again in my chin.

»Yes Tommy, I also love you. And miss by now I do you. I would take you, but there one may take no animals. Think of it Tommy, real friends know times of the separation, however, also times of the reunion.«

Our friendship requires something in pain, however, also it is ready to give a lot to feelings. Therefore it is difficult to separate me from my animals, particularly as we maintain three a tender comradeship. We also get on without many words, the animals together, also with ourselves. It is as if I stood at the moment in a full space and shout after body forces, but nobody looks to me. However, as long as the judgment is not spoken yet, I will enjoy the suture of my animals even more intensely.

1.9 The negotiations

The next days passed relatively normally. I can hardly still remember the questioning and also I had totally forgotten the lawyer in the meantime. Rex has become a dear dog, plays regularly with Tommy who enjoyed having a playfellow completely in his suture.

Mostly to the ailment of my flowers, there took her catch finish playing and with invested ears, the tail between the hind legs stuck and the head hanging, they accepted her telling-off. However, few minutes later, everything was forgotten again and the next flowers about which sealing works exist bent broken towards ground.

At the beginning I had despaired when Rex transformed the garden into a lunar landscape because he buried too with pleasure his toys. An instinctive behavior to hide his property from other robbers. Probably he has buried them before Tommy, because only when both close friends became, the avoidable gardening stopped.

Today I take pleasure every day of my both animals, the playing time with Rex on the pasture enjoys where he can let off steam so properly and his excessive energy loses; make happy me if Tommy comes in the evening to bed and delivers in the middle of the night with the horizontal bar his claws in my head; and also observes too with pleasure how all both disciplines of the Olympic plays understand in the garden.

There came Saturday, one day where one can get a good night's sleep if one has no animals. Thus Tommy was once again that to which by the night-sleeping hour at half past six my face tickled so near sniff at, that his vibrissae everywhere.

»Good morning Tommy,« I spoke to him, got up and went on the terrace. The daybreak had already awoken and a new day began. Beside us seated the cat on the one hand, Rex on the other side and together we looked to the sky, enjoyed the air of the still young day. Birds trilled and sang in the highest tones. Especially nicely the little men sing, they want to draw the attention thus to themselves to like the females. A squirrel climbed a tree down and disappeared in neighbor garden.

I went in again, followed by two starved beings whose feeding bowls cannot be full enough. A habit which has got meanwhile also Rex never to eat feeding bowls blank, to let dry up rather, so that the fresh is refilled over and over again.

Early morning I went shopping and when I came back and opened the mailbox, I found a letter with simplistic certificate. Like scales it fell to me from the eyes when I held this envelope shaking in the hand. It was certainly the thing with Tommy them was to be cleared whom me possibly as an offender, rascal or killer shows.

With a knife I opened carefully the upper edge and got out writing. It was a judicial load. My face changed color crimson, my pulse caught in to race and my veins threatened to burst. I trembled in the whole body, had to stabilize for the moment placed, my hypertension to cause no choleric attacks and social devastation.

Such writings verse meadows one not only the complete week-end, but the days afterwards immediately with. Therefore took an absolutely lousy day, stamped by confusion of thought and abdominal cramps, his run. I poured out myself one of these noble cognacs and drank up him in a train. Then I decided to get drunk so properly and to smoke a cigarette after the others. At noon thus I already started with beer and with the wholesome cigarette I still had to be patient to Marc went past, because I dispose as a non-smoker of no cigarettes.

When Marc came, I already had down the third flask of beer and was to be mixed, besides, to me a vodka coke.

»If you also wanted one, I asked.«

»No thanks, still is too early for me.«

I gave him the letter of the court which he read carefully. He read him several times, he did not set aside even the legal instruction.

With a big gulp I emptied my glass and, besides, was to be poured out myself one more when Marc spoke to me:

»Say sometimes now you want to get drunk, only because you have received writing from the court? Nevertheless, this still has to mean nothing at all.«

»Oh I can vomit about the particularism. There one gets his Tommy again and is put possibly for it still in the prison.«

If one is in the middle of the drunkenness, one consciously works towards infringements, renounces the etiquette and points out to the facts that have all no notion and nobody understands one. Actually, did not feel me at all after society, however, I was not able to do loneliness, however, also. Thus Marc was just the right thing for my mental garbage.

The more I drank, the more I sank into self-pity and then it happened: I fell from the stool.

»Uffa what this is for a wind today one can hardly stand,« I murmured before myself on which Mac picked up me from the ground.

»I believe, I must still drink what.«

»One, I believe rather you has to go in the bed, before you still hit somewhere with the skull.«

»Häää?!? Hick what is with the skull whip?«

»Man Gerard what you mumble to you there together one understands no word.«

»This is nobody mumble colleague, this is the alcohol! Thrown away money is got drunk half, finally.«

Marc took off me, laid me in the bed and immediately I fell asleep.

There came the day where I had to go to the court. My friend Marc accompanied me, sat in the auditorium, between the other curious audiences.

It was a usual courtroom, as well as one knows him from features. In the head a woman with black evening gown. Their make-up cases seemed to exist only of white powder and black eyeliner and the hair had bound them to a bun. On the right the public prosecutor, also black dressed with a furious look which taught fearing already from wide ones. On the left side my lawyer, also with black coat-like garment. Beside him I sit, the defendant, the fluorescent central figure of every process, the central figure of negotiations.

The crime is a fulcrum and pivot of the events, and according to proof position, ability of the defender one is either guilty or not guilty. The remorse, the sad dachshund's look to the judge and to the public prosecutor is decisive also for a mild judgment.

Before the judge a table with chair for the loaded witnesses. The public prosecutor left the indictment:

»Defendant, to them is accused of having penetrated deliberately with primitive power into the barn and of having broken open the castle of a grid box there with the help of a crowbar destructively to appropriate a cat illegally. They have made themselves guilty with it of the severe theft on which I demand a punishment of five years.«

My defender knocked with his fingertips on my wrist, a gesture which admonishes to the rest. As a result there spoke the judge:

»Defendant, do they feel guilty for this action?«

»But please, this they do not believe yourself!«

»What I believe or not, I decide!« As a result my defender took the floor:

»What my mandator wanted to say with it, is that he doubts the procedure and appeals therefore around adjustment. I join to him.«

The negotiations took his run. There came witnesses whom I had never seen before in my life, probably witnesses the circumstances certain against cash payment in the right direction steer.

Then the psychologist who had sounded out me before and believed now at last that I would be better lifted in the prison. However, my lawyer tried to calm me over and over again, while he laid his fingertips beating on my wrist over and over again.

At the end the judgment was announced by the judge what tore me totally from the socks:

»The court assumes from the fact that we deal here with an extremely dangerous person. Who maintains just the thought to add to every ailment which makes a mistake to his cat, is a danger for the general public. The defendant is violent and belongs under control of a prison. Herewith I announce a term imprisonment of five years without proving. The negotiations are closed.«

While the judge hit with his hammer several times on his writing desk, I jumped up and shouted straight through the courtroom:

»I AM NOT VIOLENT!«

Immediately two watchmen attacked here, my arms turned to the back and pressed my upper part of the body the table. With closed eyes I tried to defend myself to free myself from this arrest, shook me with all the strength to and fro, tried to remove my body of the table to release, however, all strains and efforts me from the power, failed.

Then I felt warm, softy hand by my hair went, affectionately along my cheek glided and calmed me. Slowly I opened my eyes and a beam of light which broke by the clouds, my heart fulfils with the sun. It was the magic one sparkle of the sky-blue eyes of my Eva, my beloved woman who looked at me and stroked my face.

She spoke and her voice sounded like a music instrument, are fine, clear and sounding, creamy and was roguish empathetically, and consider; sounded like cream tastes, before it melts on hot chocolate and thus I heard gentle words, the aforesaid ones:

»Honey, you wear dreamt, awake!«

All of a sudden I woke up, put me upright, rubbed to me the eyes and considered. Was really only one dream?

»Where is Tommy,« I asked after a while.

»He lies in the sitting room in his little bed and sleep. Why do you ask?«

»I have dreamt …, dreamt that Tommy was pinched …, from animal catchers.«

I told the story in a short representation, from breaking open the castle, this fetch back from Tommy, the present before the door, the appearance of Rex, the summons in court and the judgment of five years of prison.

Rest entered, one moment of the consideration. Then after a short break I further spoke:

»Say sometimes, do we have, actually, Marc in our neighborhood? A Mrs. Susebier? A basset?«

»Not I would know,« replied my woman.

It was all only one dream, a psychic activity during the sleep, a lively experience accompanying with images, a trip in the shallows of the soul and their phobias.

2. From Tom's micron view

2.1 My new home

It was spring before some years when I came into the world. My eyes were still closed and I could orientate myself only by the odor of my mommy and my brothers and sisters. As latest from myself to three ones I always had to fight for my place in the crib, so that I do not starve.

One day such a neighbor whom they addressed over and over again with Gerard visited at all my master. He glided with a finger over my back and a high feeling originated. It was as if the snow had melted long ago, single birds to themselves a few insects got in racket and the postman whistled a happy song, it was like spring which flowed by me through. However, after a short time he stopped with him stroke again.

He gave sounds of himself which I did not understand, like a meow which was changed up to the unappreciative. However, his acoustic language was soft and gentle.

The days passed and there came the time where I could see sudden. I saw the first time my mommy how she lay there on the side and stretched to me her nipples against. Mommy looked good, had black back fur and a white abdomen. Also the feet were white and mommy had quite long vibrissae, so beard hair as well as I, only is mine a lot, much shorter.

I looked different a little bit, had thus a brownish fur, not at all like mommy, but exactly like they a white abdomen. Also my brothers and sisters had white abdomens and also white feet, only the rest was differently colored.

Often I played with my tail, tried to catch him always, however, he was still so small, and I did not get at him.

The neighbor was there again, from recently which had stroked me so fantastically. He observes me and drivels at all so a weird stuff that I did not understand. Mommy understands a little from the sounds and had translated. Then he caught again to me to stroke, to glide with the fingertip about my back. It was so pleasant ones that I had to make a hump to feel it even better.

Then my master something spoke of Loris who would soon belong to him or should talk thus and which he with me. But, nevertheless, I do not understand him if he talks with me. He should learn maybe for the moment the meow, then purring, growling, hiss and hissing, could communicate we excellently with each other.

Two days later was there again, this "Gerard" and thus I meowed mommy in, to wake up and to translate to me what about me thus everything tells. However, mommy went on sleeping, I jumped at them and immediately she snapped at me to make something so not once more.

»Believe mommy, mommy, I, they speak of me. What want from me.«

»Boy, it is soon the time where you must stand on own feet. Then you will leave me and build up your own life, in a home where you it identifies will well have. Also to your brothers and sisters the same destiny will go out, it is the run of our life.«

I was deflected by the snap of the fingers of the "Gerard", went, sniffed in it and let me from him do the crawl. Maybe he is that with I should live, then am can visit me close to mommy and them always. Oh this was nice if he pulled his fingertips about my back, it prickled in the whole body as feelings of happiness flowed out by one through.

He let himself stroke time, did not stop at all with him, however, sometime I became tired and went to mommy. In her warm breast I fell asleep immediately.

The next day master took my mommy, my brothers and sisters and me, laid us in a basket and left.

»Mommy,« I shouted, »where do we drive?«

»You must be not afraid, we go only to the doctor. This is only to our well-being, if we are ill that one makes us again Healthy.«

Master spoke with the doctor and as well as mommy had understood, everything is with us in order, only with me one had appeared to a cat's girl, but I am a cat. Whether this had anyhow influence on my future, nobody could say, at least mommy also did not know.

Humph, cat or hangover where is there the difference? My brothers and sisters just look like me or how mommy. I have never seen dad, unfortunately. Mommy has only sometimes told about him how they have become acquainted as they raved on a farm in the hay and went together on the hunt. How he had tangled with bigger cats around mommy to protect. Often they have looked with each other to the moon and have thought to a common future.

One morning he went on the hunt for mice and came never again. Mommy said, she was very sad, was alone, nobody on her side. Then days later we came into the world and mommy became the single cat's mother. I believe mommy dad has very much, very much with pleasure had.

»It becomes a time that we say goodbye. Tomorrow master brings you to this Gerard. He lives not far from here, you will have it absolutely well with him. Your brothers and sisters are brought the day after tomorrow in a new home that lies, however, a little bit farther, as well as I had understood it.«

I was a little sad, however, on the other hand I had a good feeling with Gerard. He emits thus a warm mercy, Seemed like animals and as well as mommy told, he has fallen in love with me. What also has to mean this.

The next day came and I had to go again in this basket. My still-master took me and together with his wife they went on foot to this Gerard. I looked by the bars of the basket, noticed to me the way, every single tree, every property to be able to run back if necessary again if I did not like it.

Then we stood before his door and noticeably I felt a little fear not to know fear what lay now before me. The door rose and immediately I heard his voice which was quite confidential to me. However, I understood not a single one sound again what the people babbled there under themselves. Mommy was not there anymore which could help now.

They put me with the basket on the ground of the hall, opened the wicker door and laid a filthy lobe besides. Then they disappeared somewhere down. It was quiet, only now and again I heard voices from there resounding below up. What make me now only, could run out of the basket and hide me where differently, only where, I do not know a lot here. Thus I remained for the moment in the basket and waited.

Gerard, my new masters came up, looked to me in the basket and as a result disappeared fast again. Creeping I crept for the wicker orifice, the stair saw still like he down went and thus I ran fast in another space, before he comes again. It seemed to be the sitting room, I examined for the moment every corner, looked for a suitable hiding place.

Suddenly I heard steps again. Quick I ran behind the couch, pricks up my ears and listened. This shuffle of the feet stopped in the hall, was quiet for one moment and then moved again back down.

Tiredly I became, only wanted to sleep. A strenuous day came to an end for me. My eyes closed and already I was in the dream again with mommy.

Suddenly I woke up when in the hall sounds were given by themselves. A door opened and the sounds to be heard became quieter and quieter. Then the door shut again and I heard only a Tabs, Tabs, and Tabs. Again a door rose and again to, then another on and it became Quiet.

Once more my eyes closed and I proceeded on a dream trip in the cat's sky.

Sometime I woke up, was hungry. Thus I crept behind the sofa out and went on the search for what for eatable ones. In the kitchen dished plates stood fully with salmon and trout, as well as with cheese full Brekkies. Tasty and thus I devoured almost everything.

However, then I had to pee, the kitchen, hall, the sitting room and dining room, as well as parts of the being open bedroom combed. However, nowhere a loo and the pressure became bigger and bigger. In the sitting room in the corner I could not hold it any more, it shot like Fontaine from me out.

Made easier I walked to the terrace door, looked by the disk outward and saw the illuminated garden. My future empire, I imagined. It was slowly getting light and there I already hear like my new master the bedroom ran. Immediately I crept away behind the curtain, looked under the free piece between ground and curtain through and saw how master came to the sitting room. He looked in the corner, then came up hotfoot to me, knelt down and minced with the finger before my nose to and fro.

He wanted to play with me, I found this good and thus I tried to catch the finger what I managed quite well, because I was fast-reacting and was turned. However, then he reached for me, laid me in his bending and fondled my abdomen. Hmmm, could have gone on for hours it so. I purred satisfaction and, besides the saliva from the mouth on his shirt went on to me drop by drop, however, the interested master not, that did the crawl.

All at once we were in a space which I did not know yet. It was the bathroom which put on one side five degrees down. Here stood my toilet in which I was put in and could do now extensively my business.

The way catch I already alone back, stair out, by the kitchen, by the hall in the sitting room. There knelt my new master and was to be removed, besides, my incontinence. Beaming with delight I jumped him immediately in the heels, further wanted to play, get, hide, catch all the same what, and simply play. Master took the time and thus we raved quite long with each other, until I became tired. There he took me with both hands and laid me in my bed, in my own bed, I had own bed.

Startled I jumped up when I heard an acoustic signal that sounded like a fanfare. Immediately I buried myself behind the couch, there I felt fairly sure. Forwards it was plentiful burst, to the back just so much and upwards the back support was directly on the wall.

Master opened a door and again the sounds which I could not interpret were to be heard, unfortunately! It was a person whom I did not know yet that I heard in the voice. They went anyhow down on which it would become quiet. After a while I came out behind the sofa and the curiosity packed me what could be there below that they disappear there.

Thus I crept extremely slowly through the dining room, hall, kitchen, and the stair down and landed in the other rooms which had the appearance of a bar. My master an unknown man stood behind a separation similar to table such, before it. I shut to master, tried to bite in his heel on which he saw all at once anyhow happily down, me picked up and other told:

»This is Tommy, my new occupant.«

I heard so often "Tommy" whether is this a name for me? How I was with mommy still, there had shouted me always with Lori. Peculiarly! Lori - Tommy, Tommy – Lori!

2.2 Mommy comes for visit

Weeks and months passed. I had met it here really well, got tasty things to eat, had immensely many toys, could act and let his what I wanted and learnt fast to interpret the sounds of master. Mostly, however, I acted in such a way as if I did not understand him. However, this deals nothing with disinterest, it is only my theatrical talent I wants to prove to act so as if I did not understand it, so that master fills more interesting.

In the morning if he comes from the bathroom, my feeding bowls are filled for the moment. Not I am hungry, now I have hunger already, only the food what master presented, am so tasty that one must treat it like a flask of good wine. After opening for the moments allow to "breathing" extensively, so that it can unfold his full aroma by the contact with oxygen. Just as my food that on decanting his total taste develops.

Then I must keep to my engagements. First the direct neighbor whom I reach with a jump about the partition wall. She always waits and has constantly a handful Brekkies for me ready. Also the next neighbor pauses quite longingly and receives me with a tasty dose feed.

Behind it there lives a man, which has animals the wings have and with it can fly. First I did not like him because he never permitted to me that I play to catch with the plumage. I would also have handled quite warily with the animals, although it would not have looked here and there afterwards. However, then I have understood it.

These are the things which sometimes have another existence form, but especially well are treated because these are friends. Just as my master and me are good friends. He looks after and maintains them, gives them what to scoff and always has a sleeping place for them ready. These are his kinds of "cats".

I ignored since then the plumage of him, held only almost every day a vast nap in his Hollywood swing, so that I could visit afterwards rested mommy.

Mommy is glad whenever I come and I must always tell her everything till the smallest detail what I have experienced so during the day and how it would go out to me home so. I live already very long with my new master and mommy hears every day the same history. I believe mommy becomes old, forgets a lot, maybe she also has Alzheimer or in such a way.

»I am glad that you have met it so well.

Your master is a really nice person. Since you are from the house, my little woman and my master look even more after me. Sometimes think I that they expect younger generation from me again, however, for something like that I feel too old a little. From your brothers and sisters I have heard long nothing more, but to those it also goes well so far, I hope at least.«

»Mommy, you always tell the same one. They will have this quite well, makes to you about that no head.«

»Do you mean?«

»M-u-m-m-y! Visit me rather sometimes, as you have promised it to me so often. My master will be glad certainly about it. Then I must not always tell you again like it with myself looks, then sees it sometimes same. Your thick mate who visits you always can come along if he feels like.«

»Yes, yes, we can see sometimes.«

»Not yes yes, if tomorrow you do not come, I get you!«

»Yes I will come.«

»So mommy, I have to go now further, the other neighbors visit, they already wait certainly.«

»Vouch sometimes you think this that you

eat through everywhere? I think you get from your master always so much?«

»Yes, already. But it has become anyhow already a sort of customary law to visit the neighbors and if they to me what to eat put, then, nevertheless, I cannot reject it. This would amount to insults and are disappointing, you have always said me, and one is allowed to do nobody. So mommy, think of it and do not disappoint you me, soon visit with me!«

These were really of all nice people I visited. Some gave me name which I could not soberly pronounce sometimes, like Schnucki, pussy or Catty. Others knew even my right name: Tommy.

Days passed and mommy had not visited me, as well as she had promised it.

Today was a marvelous morning when I stood on the terrace. The sun already seemed about the horizon and only isolating clouds in the sky obstructed her wide way to the earth to the warm rays. I got on the way to make my everyday respects and was about midday again with mommy. The thick cat next door, was there also and both looked at me, as if they already expected me.

»So mommy, shows today I you sometimes my garden. Finishes you, now it goes off.«

»Oh no, one leaves, today I would not want, maybe tomorrow or the day after tomorrow.«

»Nothing, t-o-d-a-y! Always you do not feel like it. You must move sometimes a little bit more, come out sometimes of your environment, and not only always lie here in the garden. Now you come along and with it enough!«

Obediently they followed me, also the thick cat with which mommy got on very well because it is probably the only one which visits them regularly. I do not know at all what they to him finds. Though it looks very stately, however, is a cat which can eat constantly.

»Oh, you have this, however, smartly here, with garden pond. There fish are in it, red fish.«

»This is a goldfish, one may do mommy, to those nothing, only consider, and do not give a hand. I procure sometimes what to eat. Masters see what time thus in the house has.«

»M-i-i-i-a-a-a-u, M-i-i-i-a-a-a-u, master we are hungry!«

Master came, looked a little surprised and spoke whether I had brought visit. Yes, hello? Do look like adrenalin tourists who look for dangerous graceful attractions, or how?

While mommy observed the fish in the pond, the thick cat could not behave once more and peed in the botany.

»Say sometimes one has hunted you with the scrubbing brush by the nursery or why do you pee on my sunbathing area?«

»Excuse me, it seems never again,« he spoke very cautiously, lay there like a starfish and the first time I noted how shyly this lion of cat was real. The reason for his mysterious behavior, is unknown to me. Maybe the fear of people, none him loves or that nobody looks after him, only mommy.

I ran master behind here, showed him the way and the cupboard where my feed was to be found. After a while he was ready, everything stacked on a tray and brought a huge number of bowls out on the terrace. Immediately we rushed at the delicacies. Alternately we ate from everybody bowl, everywhere something else was in it. It was like food in a Chinese turntable where every guest turns the desired food to himself, only with the difference that we had to turn on the dishes.

The foods were richly and absolutely satisfying, however, half remained lying.

Even of the thickness everything had not finished, also seemed to be full, at least up to the next mouthful.

Successively we caught to ourselves to clean, not we are personal care fanatics, no it lies in the nature of our forefathers, always well to looks, to be clean to curry the fur regularly. For it we have an especially rough tongue, with the so small hooks which clean the fur then like a brush.

Suddenly mommy caught to me in the head to leak. »You must clean yourself in fact, there everywhere is still get dirty,« she cried.

»Mommy I is no small kitten, I am able to do this completely alone, hear on with it.«

»Earlier you would like this.«

»Yes earlier, there I was still small and clumsy, now I am big and wash me to hundred spots on the day.«

Oh this was embarrassing for me to let clean me before the thick cat of my mommy. He thinks, nevertheless, certainly, I am a mommy's boy, a tear-swollen mommy child, a weakling of the virtue.

»So mommy is good now. I believe I bring you now rather again home.«

We started to run and master something still shouted behind me what I did not understand, however, any more.

2.3 Behind grids

The next days passed, as usual, up to one day. There a man was in the front garden, dressed with a white smock. He looked peaceful and friendly, squatted down as him me saw and rustled Brekkies.

My almost insatiable curiosity, combined with an eccentric compulsion to the thirst for knowledge, did me to step closer the stranger. Stroking he wore out my fur and laid, besides, over and over again a Brekkies before my nose. A nice guy, I imagined, a neighbor? Actually, I know them all, she visits regularly on my early morning walk, but this here, and those do not know me yet.

However, then suddenly he reached in my nape, as well as mommy it always did when she carried us babies in the mouth to and fro. I caught in to hiss, to hiss dreadfully in, because I knew all at once that what he nothing good acted is becomes.

He had said silly cattle to me when he raised me in the nape fur, silly cattle to me. I am no silly cattle, everybody can confirm this here in the neighborhood. I am dear because they all are nicely to me. Hissing I tried to let feel him my claws, however, he held me too far from his body distant, so that I could not reach him.

The second guy opened the carriage door, took me and mended me into a cage. Fury and fear before what will come controlled my feelings. Steam collects, an explosive attack which could sprinkle in the vicinity of fifteen meters of car in the air. I could have bent bars if I was Rambo; if fear could give on account of my descent to the guys if one recognizes me as a B.A. of the A team and as a MacGyver I would make from shit honey if I owned the ability. However, I am kidnapped only one cat is stolen who at this moment robbed, am kidnapped, is taken away by force.

I had to think of mommy, hopefully they do not kidnap mommy. This would not survive them. Mommy is quite old and does not bear excitement at all, however, actually, she never comes down from her property. But what is if mommy wants to visit me now on own initiative, me surprise and possibly to these guys in the hands falls …,

… I have to go here out!

With all the strength I ran against the cage, tried to gnaw the sticks by, squeezed my head through, however, everything was in vain. The car drove a long distance, then it bumped above a way that I was lifted constantly in the winds and then he stopped.

A man got out. I listened, he went a few steps, opened anyhow a door, a big door. The carriage went on afterwards, stopped shortly after again and the engine was switched off. The other man got out.

In the extreme corner of the cage I crept away and behaved quite quietly, wanted to listen what happens there. The rear door rose and one of these men got. He opened my cage door and put a substantially smaller one before it. Then he did me with a floor from the corner, so that I run in the other cage. However, I fell over and over again on this floor, defended myself with all claws were available to me. However, soon I was fed up them to feel constantly the bat on my back and ran in the other cage.

It was narrow here, could hardly move me, almost the soul from the body hissed to me.

When I looked around, I noted that I was in an extremely big space, a hall or barn. Before me a generally barred separation, a kennel. So one neighbor, there sleeps also has one always his dog in it. An old ramshackle dog with extremely short bones and the much too long ears which sharpened constantly along the ground. In the head he had a white blaze and his expression is constantly sad with particularly grown tired lachrymal sacs.

While one opened the door of this grid house, the other opened the bolt in my cage and shook as long as, until I fell from the narrow cage. Hissing I am replied act, caught in to growl to demonstrate to him my challenge

Both guys disappeared and left alone me. Fiercely I looked to them behind, until they closed the gate behind themselves.

I was locked up, caught in a totally barred cage, far by my master and my mommy. What I have done that I am here what want from me. Nevertheless, I am only quite a normal cat, nothing special. Suddenly I saw in a corner two other cats, two female cats, completely frightened, am worried, frighten and timorously.

»Hello, My name is Tommy. What is this here where we are here?«

»I am Lisa,« mentioned one. »It is nothing good here, we are used to the testing of some things. What, however, exactly, I do not know.«

»I have belonged of it already on occasion,« contacted the other to word. She seemed to be older and experienced, possibly has the better view.

»The experiments serve only the people, many of us have not come back from such excursions any more. Others were suddenly seriously ill, nobody knew why.«

It seemed to me everything very peculiarly, at the same time I did not understand the sense and purpose, why one should use us just for a test. However, I also had to attack no desire other thoughts. I knew only one, I must find a possibility to come here out.

As a cat one is marked in the society of the female cats to provide for protection and to fight for a freeing. This wants to and today should be confirmed. Thus I spoke a little bit affected:

»I will find a possibility to come here out.«

»How you want to make this, look around. The bars are so narrow that just one paw fits through. And if you look sometimes upwards, you see that there also everything is wired in.«

»Yes, nevertheless, but there must be a possibility to come here out?«

»Law the case, we find a possibility to come out here where do we have to go there? Do you know where we have landed here?«

»Is right, you are right! But I know one and there I am sure by hundred percent, my master will search me and he will find me. He will find me everywhere, I know this.«

»But how should find you here, here somewhere, no notion where we are!«

»My master will think me that I swear you. Absolutely he is already on the search and my thoughts will accompany him. Only wait, he will come.«

I saw the skepticism in their faces what was understandably for me, because how my master should find me also here. However, one may not lose hope, must give to faith, and protect optimism.

Longing climbed up in me, longing for my master. What I would do only everything to be now with him, to cuddle up to him, to feel his hand on my back.

The night ran quietly, except that to eat we what and waters to the drinking agreed, nothing happened. Also no other cats came to us.

We three did not have to say ourselves a lot, waited for an opportunity to flee, however, the guys were clever. If they eat brought, they never left open the grid door, shooed away us before in a corner, before they put bowls purely.

Again I thought of my master, thought about what he would probably make now. Since we live together, this night was the first one which everybody had spent for itself. An unusual situation. What probably think the neighbors whom I cannot visit and mommy what thinks mommy only if I do not come. Oh, I may not remember at all.

The barn gate rose, a man entered, rose in the carriage and drove out him backward. Then the gate was closed again.

»They go again on predatory attack, want to catch even more cats,« spoke Mizzi, older of the both.

»Now we could dig a hole under the grid,« contacted Lisa to word.

»This has identified no sense. Dogs dig with pleasure and for reason one lets in grid in general a little piece in the surface of the earth,« answered Mizzi.

One well did not come that the proposal from me, also did not know because that one digs grid in the ground. There I would have disgraced myself quite a lot.

2.4 The escape assistant

The waiting became eternity, nothing brought me to it to something to ways to bring. My life ran at the moment bores and half-heartedly. Everything became no matter to me, whether uncleansed fur, thick sandy punches in the eyes or vegetarian food. Apathy spread, a trait of the circumstances and events accepts without valuing this particularly. Phrases like >being able to do you make as you want<, or >jacket like trousers<, or >is to me, nevertheless, sausage< rose with by the head.

However, then I had to think again of master, to my dad. What he will make in such a way, without me. Nevertheless, I was it which made him every morning long before the alarm clock awake; his newspaper in such a way prepared, as if it freshly came from the shredder; itself basically in the laundry basket to the clean laundry laid because it still was warmly from the dryer; with the letter write the fountain pen led; he brought the laptop to a blue screen with hexadecimal and mistake codes which slept in flowerpots and uses the cat's grass as a sunbathing area.

Also it was my job to provide for the meticulous cleanness of my master and to lick off his face to him regularly what went best of all if he slept.

What will make master only without me. I was discouraged and not was sad sadly at the same time, because I white whether I become reunions him. This separation means ailment for me. He has his job, his friends, however, I have only him be in me the plant trust on which I live.

I fell asleep and dreamt, dreamt of our games, of our mutual banter, from the catch and raving, from hiding and attacking, from sleeping and also being lazy.

Often he spoke with me and if I also did not understand his words, thus, nevertheless, his voice which turned to me. Sometimes he was also angry, but only one short moment, then he stroked me again.

Suddenly I woke up, a bruit, a car was to be heard. Everybody three we squatted in the corner and waited on what will happen.

The gate rose and the car went purely. The man slammed loudly the carriage door and left loudly calling the barn. Clattering he closed the gate behind himself and it became quiet again.

Few minutes later the gate rose again and one of these men approached. He saw us in the corner crouching together, opened carefully our grid door and put quite fast a bowl with food and water purely. Then he disappeared again. Everybody at the same time we set about it to the bowls and sniffed. It smelt anyhow unpleasantly, did not correspond that what served master to me. Moreover, all that hit to me on the stomach, simply had no hunger. Thus I took only one some from the water and went afterwards in stooped position again to the corner. I was sad, extremely sad.

However, then I heard voices, hardly perceptible voices. They were mild, more whispering, and a breath of whispering whispering. The wind was too strong outdoors, falsified the sounds, so that only the helping came.

Who was this, I imagined what run there for people to and fro or these are his accomplices who bring other animals?

I further listened, concentrated upon the vocal position, on which what is talked there with which sound and which accent whether these are bad or good people and then I recognized them, the voice. It was that of my master, it was my master which stood outdoors and with somebody extremely quietly I talk could not see him because the transporter kept me the view to the aperture, but I was sure hundred per that it was the voice of my master.

»I have said it you,« I murmured to the other cats. »I have said it you, my master will come and there he is, there at the window. He will get out to us everybody here, my master.«

Luck feelings penetrated me, feelings of happiness I feel because I know that my thoughts have landed with him. The emptiness which one feels which unusual, if one misses somebody is felt. I cannot describe my joy, but master will know it, he shows such things always.

I peeped under the carriage through, could see his bones and his hand which touched the ground. He went to the transporter and by the side disk and windscreen I could see his face how he turned on the light of the car. Well people have a problem in the darkness, they can see not so well, as we.

Short time later master came out behind the carriage and called me and from then on I knew, everything becomes good again. He has found me, my dad. Forever we will be connected to each other, from now on this is certain.

He glided with his hand over my head, about my back, oh how I had the missing, but now he is there, now he will get me.

Master needed tools, he said to me to

release me, because the kennel was closed. I saw like, however, he searched nothing found. Then somebody called in from outdoors and also the voice seemed to me close, however, she could not identify yet properly. Master put out the light in the car, crept fast under the carriage and at the same moment the gate of the barn rose.

One of these hooligans came in, went along our kennel to another corner. Now opportunity would be to be crept up for master from the back and to resolve pitilessly him, to carry him with punches in the offside, to point, what it means Tommy to pinch.

However, he remained lying under the carriage, did not stir. Well, he will already have a reason, at least, however, I know that my dad there is to be released around me.

The man disappeared again and after one moment master also came under the carriage out tickled. He has to go back tools get, soon is again, he said and disappeared once more by the windowless orifice.

I lay there and saw to him behind, saw under the carriage as his feet disappeared up. It became quiet again to say nobody been capable something.

The time passed and nothing did itself.

Also outdoors nothing was to be heard, only the light rushing of the lukewarm wind in the trees. I had to think again of my master where he probably was now or possibly the crooks have caught him? Why does he keep waiting me here so long?

»What is then with the freeing action of your master? If was probably a complete waste of effort or you see him here somewhere. He has probably got the trousers full and has cleared out.«

Mizzi, the dressed up old goat, tried badly about my master here move, but not with me! Horrific that the fur stood to her to mountains, I spitted at them; made a hump that it stepped back anxiously, shut to them and spoke with vigorous sounds:

»My master will come, you will see. And if you tries once again to doubt the credibility my masters, then pay attention well to you!«

»I have not meant it, nevertheless, in such a way, but he is away for a long time, nevertheless, would have to be long time ago again here.«

»Maybe something has interfered, simply waits, he will already come,« I hoped at least.

2.5 Rescue approaches

It sounded, as if it rained outdoors. The sky must be overcast with clouds which allowed to splash now fleecy water to ground what is soaked up then greedily by the earth around new life to create.

People are, actually, scared of water beings, already hide with the first drop under shade-donating umbrellas or cover themselves with all kinds of waterproof things. Also we cats like not necessarily water, only sometimes to the drinking.

»We will perish here miserably,« spoke Lisa sobbing.

»No,« I replied to her. »We will already come out here, I know this! Believe me this!«

The rain seemed to become stronger and stronger, more and more water beat from the sky on the earth and transforms ways into an auburn mud scenery. Puddles will line up themselves and be filled malleolus-deeply with brackish water.

Like drum beats it drums on the metal roof about us, how the drum vertebra of a drummer in a wind orchestra. At some places the rain broke through, formed small puddles in which drops hopped mincing in, again up jumped and then burst. A Weather, where I myself in it doubt whether my master comes back.

Few time later I heard how the dog barked who had to give up his home, so that we could be interned. He barked and barked and barked, until one of both rascals came out and got angry violently with him. Then it was quiet.

The gate was opened and the absolutely frightened dog was hunted in. Immediately we started everybody to hissed, made a hump to intimidate him substantially by our size, however, he passed apathetically and uninterestedly the kennel. Cooing bruits accompanied him on his way by the barn. He searched sniffing everything, until he thought a place where he lay down and his back started to lick off.

It became quiet again, nothing was to be heard. The dog had lain down on the side and slept. After a little while I heard a voice which called a name, a name I just still heard from one of the crooks. It was the name of the dog, Rex. The dog pricks up the ears, ran to an aperture and caught in quietly to howl, as if he answered whispering.

What this has to mean, I asked myself who creeps in this time by the area, only to visit a dog. It rains in streams and above all, it is pitch-dark there outdoors.

Almost everybody has already experienced this, at night in a badly illuminated area. Easily there drizzles the rain. One hurries along the street and suddenly hears steps behind himself. They approach and immediately one accelerates his own step, the distance tries to increase not to be caught up. Adrenalin, fear, horror spreads in the body, every fiber of the body is tightened, the thought of power, raids, criminal activity undresses. Some change the side of the street, however, one is only contented if one has reached the familiar home.

However, then I recognized my master again, my master had come back to get me. Under the transporter through I saw his bones, his shoes and trousers which were afflicted from humid mud. He squatted down and caught to the dog to stroke.

I stared over and considered. What does master deal with the dog, why he is so nice to him? Do you maybe know yourselves? I shook off all thoughts of myself which could deliver a negative judgment which would put me in the background.

However, I was too curious and peeped once more under the transporter through. He still stroked the dog, why only? What do they have with each other? Nevertheless, I am that who would have to be stroked; he was kidnapped; one had robbed and had taken away by force. I need comforting strokes, the proof that dad still loves me. The dog is only one enemy, belongs, finally, to the rascals!

Master laid his flashlight so on the ground that it shone under the car through with directly in the face. The glistening light dazzled so much that I turned round and saw to both other cats that lay like wool hank in the corner.

»Well, too much promised? Even in bad weather my master will avoid no trouble and need to save me.«

»Braggart,« I hardly heard saying perceptible from Mizzi.

When I turned round again, master had opened just the castle, opened the door, came in and picked up me. Oh this was nice to feel his hand about my fur, to perceive his voice which spoke so nicely and softly to me, the odor his perfume mixed with the scent of the filthy mush which the rain caused ones had.

Then the dog obstructed to us the way from this cage on which I started to hiss aggressively and aggressively. With my delivered, extremely sharp claws I tried to hit after in to bore them painfully in his body. An appeal to his conscience that to him fears should intimidate.

However, master kept me other actions, believed he would be a friend, a friend ready to help. He passed me by the orifice and there was the other whose voice I recognized, nevertheless, anyhow. It was my former master, the master of mommy, the best friend of my master, Marc. I was glad to see him, to hear to feel because I know that he was well to my mommy.

To the better one advance, Marc laid me in a basket and crept by the wood. I turned round in the basket to see where master remains, however, he did not come and soon we were except reach, so that I did not see to scales any more.

Suddenly we stopped. Marc ducked and after short while he decreased again. Then I saw how my dad met us, with him the stupid dog. What does want master with him?

Marc and my master spoke for a while together, quite quietly and waited. I had luck which was thick roof of this basket, so that no rain walked in, but the drops which bounced off on master's jacket over and over again hit between the bars through. My fur was quite really humid and the basket was too small to clean me upright.

I hate water, I simply do not like it. It makes itself scarce me nastily and. The prettiness factor sinks rapidly if I am wet and nobody looks at me more, not sometimes mommy.

»If we cannot hurry up a little, I am quite drenched,« I meowed, however, nobody answered, only one "Pssssst", I heard.

The dog started sniffing in my box, then sniffed in master's things and then again in my box. To show him in his barriers, I spitted at him for the moment dreadfully exciting, so that he knows who man is here. Finally, it has also helped in Mizzi.

As a result the dog bent his head a little to side and looked at me expectantly. Again I spitted at him, even more menacingly, even more dangerously and even more cunningly like before.

»Pssssst, Tommy is quiet,« I heard again and after a while of the rest we went on.

Then I saw master his car. Then I saw master his car. Silver the colored Ford which is at least as old as mommy today. Often I have run towards him if he went on the court. Be I recognized clattering engine noise already from wide one.

In a great hurry everybody got and I was glad about the fact that the dog stayed behind. Atmospheric friends climbed up in me, because it goes home and tomorrow I must teach for the moment mommy everything carefully what I have experienced everything. Absolutely she has given herself big troubles because I had not visited them yesterday.

Suddenly we stopped. Master got out and went to a telephone box. He called up, called up the police, reported about Mizzi and Lisa who are held prisoner, against her will. The conversation did not last long, then he came back again and we went on. Yes so is my master, looks even after the other cats, she simply does not let down.

At home come, I wanted to sleep for the moment so properly, laid me immediately beside master's pillow and fell asleep, while my both rescuers watered her triumphal procession still in the cellar bar.

2.6 Be free

The next day I could not come fast enough out, nevertheless, had to tell everywhere what I had experienced. First my Brekkies with the neighbor fetch and with the aunt afterwards.

Today the pigeon breeder lets out sometimes, because his birds would not understand my history as well as thus and thus I landed earlier as usual with mommy.

The thick cat was also, lay about before mommy and looked uninterestedly in the area.

»Hello, mommy, I am there again. I must tell to you sometimes a story, you will not believe it what has happened to me.«

»My boy where it was the last days I had missed you.«

»I just, nevertheless, want to tell this you, and do not interrupt me now. If you know, I was just in the front garden, was exhausted by many visits I made, wiped with the sweat of the forehead as a man on me it came up.

He had an asymmetrical formed nose which had changed color from violet to black. His look was dark, it looked very extremely bad and in his cheek bone deep grooves formed. Under the eyes hung gigantic lachrymal sacs and the second chin gushed forth from the collar of his shirt close up to the neck.

A man one looked that he brings on with the abandonment of a business, in general the electronic anti-theft device.

With some things he tried to lure me, however, I remained steadfast, walked him with my different porcelain retouchers tools, like teeth, claws, humps and my unique, unmistakable, unrestrained, crude and impressive killer look.

Other would fall of it immediately in faint, then would have to be moved into the stable side situation and agree on the left and to the right of some to the cheeks, so that they are awake on time if the rescue car comes again. However, the guy pulled no look.

Still he had to have got anyhow fear, he squatted down and stretched to me his hand against, a welcoming ritual, the explanation of a defeat or a peace offer?

Slowly I approached him to see what he held there in the hand.«

»Come to the point,« interrupted me to the thickness.

»Simply slowly,« I said on it.

»He is right,« meant mommy, »do not make it so exciting.«

»Well, this guy, reached with his exceedingly big hand quite brutally for me, pulled me with all the strength in a cage and kidnapped me somewhere there in a wilderness, completely, quite far away. There I was put completely alone on myself, I was locked up with two other cat's girls in my dungeon, however, beings have seen female actual, not the physical strength like I she has.«

»And what you then made,« mommy asked quite awfully.

»I have fought like a tiger, had to tangle even with a gigantic dog, a fighting dog with an oversized knob and sharp teeth which one can compare with bite force of a garbage press.«

»Oh boy, has not hopefully happened to you, with such a terrible being.«

»Otherwise, I would not probably be here, mommy. So and now lets me pass on. I had fought, like a berserk, tried to squeeze me by the sticks through, they with my physical strength to bend apart with my will strength to break them with the teeth to split. However, in vain, they had been made out of the hardest steel. A tunnel build, a tunnel under the grids through, however, they had rammed the grid meter-deeply into the surface of the earth to avoid such escape possibilities. I had to consider, had to go here out to put a stop to a game the criminal ring. In addition I needed help. I thought quite firmly of my master, wished nothing the more ardent, than to have him now with me, so that we could put a stop to a game together the criminals. And then he came.«

»You the phenomenon controls telepathy? If I have young am so proud of you.«

»The just true arts which up to now nobody has discovered put yes mommy, in me. But at least there came my master and also your master, mommy, and thus we could take unnoticed the flight.

»Yes now mommy, in me the just true arts which still nobody had discovered is. But at least there came my master and also your master, mommy, and thus we could take unnoticed the flight.«

»Your master has got you from it? Cool!« mentioned the thick cat. »And what has become with the other cats, has it taken to her?«

»Them we leave there, exactly like the dog, but we have sent immediately the police there, so that it clears up there sometimes. Finally, we cannot do everything for them.«

Mommy was really proud of me, gave me a feeling of the big satisfaction, the respect of itself; the joy those of the certainty arises something special to have acted recognition value and future-laden.

Well, a little chauvinism and a little bit on "Poser" make my self-confidence also strengthens. Still she admired me, particularly my courage to walk towards the fear; my courage to put me to all challenges and to do my determination, things of those one is not persuaded that one gets over them regardless of.

With an intoxicated enthusiastic look the thick cat observed me, made me the hero against the will, to a superhero mutate.

With thanks I accepted his latent gestures which left me self-confidently, good-looking and intelligently appeared.

When I came home, master was totally excited, leafed chaotically round a newspaper and called up, besides, mommy's master. An article rich in sense in the newspaper should report about the rescue operation. Possibly such articles should pave even ways. Master was extremely pensive and thus it was my job to cheer up him. With a jump I was on the couch and glided with my paw over his cheek. Then I showed that I love him Quite really, glided with my nose along his chin. Immediately he caught again in to smile, was glad about my presence.

»Meow, you must not be sad, nevertheless, I am there,« meowed I.

»Nevertheless, I also love you,« he answered and pressed me quite firmly to his breast. Our "man's friendship" is what quite special, something quite valuable and from the first second in where I saw him, my master to me was welcome.

Two days later he came in with a present about which I was just glad like my master. I love wrapping paper, it crackles so nicely, is soft and affectionate and one can play wonderfully with it. Particularly if it feels tempted crumpled up and it from own strength to develop again.

Master talked and gave me the noble paper which should improve in appearance optically of presents. Presently I rushed at it, on my new sparring partner to whom violent slashes make no difference in this fight arena.

However, the curve hardly defended itself, probably wanted to toady in this kind with me because he had to go that it would be about life and death. I gave up him and planned for the bag. A bag not was big enough that I could disappear in it. Still I tried out the comfort which thanked, however, with the fact that she burst at several places.

Thus I decided the fight for myself as won and went out on the terrace. Master sat in the garden chair and swung a brown humor in a glass to and fro. A peculiar ceremonial what the people make there.

Exhausted I sat down in the patch on the ground cover. They were soft and fleecy like a down cushion. I prepared for my recreational sleep, stretched myself in all directions, inhaled with quite far opened mouth deeply and when I closed him again, nevertheless, a butterfly flew past directly in my nose.

Almost he would have landed in my open mouth and would have brought me to the suffocation, this monster. Immediately I hit after him, after this beast, however, it was more skilful than I thought, hook and loops flew.

Only a small teeny-weeny advantage could preserve him from a defeat, namely the luck to be able to fly higher the luck than I can jump.

Just a little teeny-weeny advantage could him from defeat preserve, namely to fly higher than I can jump.

It is always this if this Flash harassment resembles with these damned insects, always. Every day make one the sow.

Now I must drop myself for the moment in the drunkenness of the relaxation.

2.7 Rex came

Today like every day I also visited my mommy. She lay, as usual, in her garden and observed the birds with the aviation. Only if it rains, she creeps away under chairs, tables, in the shed or they runs in the house, by the cat's valve especially built-in for them.

»Now mommy, mommy, I am famous I is in the paper.«

»How do you get on then?«

»I have belonged like my master in a telephone call told that an article in the newspaper was written about the cat's freeing.«

»Nevertheless, Yes, however, this deals nothing with you. When the other cats were released, nevertheless, you were long time ago again at home.«

»You mean, they have not reported about the mysterious scene, about my execrable capture and about my criminal power of deduction with the inevitable victory of the good about Bad?«

»Though these are current reporting's, but only with superficial information.«

»Pity and I already seemed to me, as if I climbed a stair to the sky. Well, Hamburg or

Munich, central issue Germany.«

A little bit resignedly I went home. Master was there already, the terrace door got up. I thought of the forcible kidnapping which can cause with many traumas if they fall of a high-level phase in a deep phase.

I thought just of Lisa, the small cat's lady who was with me in the cage. It would be predestined for a mental damage which originates from power from the outside. Was elegant, still young, the world and her opponents did not know yet exactly. Hopefully it goes well to her, is healthy and again in her home.

With Mizzi I give myself no troubles, it was robust, stocky and knew the life. It will better process the kidnapping, than Lisa.

I went contemplative by the sitting room and dining room and stood in the hall when I myself nearly one trauma shoot was. I believed myself not to be any more mine itself, to see everything by a filter, as if I was dazed. Like a Flashback recollections ran past all of a sudden me which restored me into a situation from which I have fled only some days ago.

In the kitchen were my masters and his friend and between the two of fighting dog with extremely sharp teeth and the extra-large mouth.

Seconds, felt hours, I stood there still. Then I put on my perfidious and scheming criminal mug; if made a hump which increased me at least around double; delivered my sharp edged claws just sharpened in the tree and walked, extremely deeply from the lung hissing, on this short hair pit bull to.

Fury and aggressions spread, two emotions one discussion with raving applause welcomed. Slowly I approached this scoundrel, everything was to be given ready to polish him the knob, however, master called me to reason.

"Tooooommmmy," spoke master. »Leave this, this is Rex and Rex here the next time will live. He is our friend …, and therefore also your friend!«

What? He should live here? I sat down and while master driveled something with the dog, I considered whether he had meant this really seriously. I looked to master, he seemed to be quite confident, and it seems to live with the threat here to mean seriously. Humph!

Thoughts spread not to be allowed to play the first violin any more, besides, I am according to the international rank order for domestic animals still the boss here. Imagination shot to me by the head, to depart and a new home to look, however, I do not leave my master simply alone. He was there always for me, has saved me, finally, also from the claws of the criminals, I also want to be there for him always. Maybe he needs me, just now.

It is the bridge, the bridge of the belonging together which has hardened indiscernibly between us, and thus I remained.

The dog slept outdoors, this was right to me, because I do not give my bed. In the morning if I turn my round, he disappeared in the house, was also so far OK, however, I had to contrive something to get rid of him.

When I came home, Rex lay in the garden and slept. Carefully and quietly I crept with to him come on, briefly sniffed to his tail, drove out my claw and hit them in his tail apex. All of a sudden I turned round and jumped with a sentence on the partition wall of the neighbor.

Rex raised half-sleepy his head, briefly looked behind me and read him then again fall. Shit, I thought. Has hoped, he will jump behind me run and about the fence. Then I would have hunted him by the next garden, until he is away so far that he does not find the way back any more. However, maybe I have also not met his tail properly.

In a big curve round him I went to the house, to the kitchen, because I was hungry. Beside my feeding bowl lay a lobe which somebody must have forgotten there. He had a repellent, bitter sour odor of boiling oil, burnt meat and a breath of master transpiration which comes only after one week without douches to the true development. I pushed away it, away from my bowl, itself the fug on my food does not transfer.

Well saturated I went again on the terrace considered how one makes a sheepdog hunt me. If I jump and he becomes wild certain like nothing good behind me run, straight through the garden, me try to catch up, always nicely the head hold up to him the puff goes out.

Thus I looked myself again into Rex to show him who is here man in the house. However, thus often I also jumped at him, him my claws showed, or also hissed, the totally dumbfounded dog got every time in embarrassment which he bridged with the fact that he scratched, his snout leaked, started to sternutation or uninterestedly in against around sniffed. Then read he his head again fall and sank into a dusk sleep.

Sometimes, however, also he turned on the back and held out to me his paws, this coward. He wants to indicate with the fact that I do not fit in his prey pattern. If we lay cats on the back, the belligerence means, then we can defend ourselves with all paws. But dogs...?

Master sat in the garden chair and observed me. Sometimes he gave certain sounds of himself which admonished me, certain things did not reprove me to make.

Thus I had to tolerate the dog welfare or evil. Actually, he did to me also nothing, was even a sorely afflicted when we were locked up in the cage. If he walked towards us cats comfortably and left even master impartially in the barn, so that I am saved from the catches of the animal thieves.

Rex seemed to get fast that I was the boss here, left me everywhere the precedence, did not eat any more from my bowl, and did not lie down also any more in my little bed what he buried with his immense body totally. He also tolerated the visit of mommy, only the thick, he would not like that thus. He rushed always immediately at the food of Rex, so that he had to chase away him constantly barking. However, sometime the thick cat also understood that foreign property is untouchable for him. Also Rex felt bit by bit that he was, actually, a harmless cat who steps aside every annoyance amply.

2.8 All only one dream

Today was again one day where master was nervous, sad and pensive, not like the days before where he seemed happy, could not sometimes keep before laughter any more. But also depress in the times of the excitement, this and in thoughts submerged of being, one may never lose hope to experience some positive.

Ruminatively he sat on the sofa, nothing knew how to start with the day, had anyhow no plan. Now it is my job to give him the feeling of the friendship that one is there simply all the same in which situation he is also.

Thus I jumped on the sofa, put me beside him and looked at him hypnotizing from the side, until he noted me. He spoke words to me which did not sound especially well which followed of a meaning, as if one wanted to do a wedge between us.

Master had to close his bones, meanwhile I wanted to lie down in the hollow. Softly he stroked my fur and it is marvelous with which devotion he this makes, it could not be more relaxed. Again I heard words which sounded softly and plaintively.

»Not be sad,« I meowed him in. »Nobody will separate the cord which connects us.«

Then a flood of hearty affection overcame me, turned me and showed my melancholy owner, how much I love him. Besides, we cats always prod with a head easily laid to side to the chin of our master. I have learnt this from mommy, it made also always with me, sometimes this also makes even today.

Of course one can wake with it also the impression, because we have glands of perfume in the cheeks that we mark our protectors with it. Well, why not, because everybody it should smell that masters and I belong together.

»I love you also,« spoke my master to myself, my five favorite words.

Then the next day's ran again normally, master was the "old" again and my contact with Rex became better and better. We played together of the more often, try to creep to us, rather he tried to get me what failed him, however, because he it never got to jump on the saving partition wall.

»Be a pig, can be fine,« I meowed to him to.

I cannot simply keep back in such cases the damage friends, it also does not want at all. On the one hand I wanted to burn him sometimes in a pot, now on the other hand I enjoy my immoderate power demonstration which I underline with a grin still, in addition.

But dogs are no bad animals, they are only ungifted. They own four bones, a head, a tail, as well as resigned traits hectic however nevertheless. As a sheepdog they were bred, equipped with high intelligence, however, this is over. The proud dog of that time is only a caricature of itself. Only the élite of these races is used as drug search dogs and is valid among congeners as snobbish idiots in the service of the state power.

However, we cats have our own head which must be put through over and over again. Moreover, we are very intelligent, learn fast and if one taught the service of the computer us, we could help by the production of the sales tax advance notification and supervise at the same time the eBay actions.

Rex still stands there below and waits that I again down jumps. However, this is the problem that basically quick on site it is and the solution where I should jump, keeps waiting.

However, then, at one moment of the inattentiveness of Rex, I jumped on the high-level patch, by the botany, about the terrace in the house. Rex followed me about the high-level patch, laid waste the botany like a sandy storm the Sahara, let of master wonderful, stately and affectionate plants mutate to headless stalk.

Immediately master caught again in to grumble about the destruction of his caring invested patch what said like he always: Sweat and strength had cost. However, in his face catch me an unbelievable grin of the relief over and over again if he saw playing together Rex and me.

It is Saturday morning and like every day I wake up my master on time, before he fails to hear the alarm clock by his deep sleep. Embedded in the snug bedchamber where no physical studies are pursued but only amnestied dreams are experienced, master looked at me for the moment reproachfully.

Because I know, that master is obliviously and sometimes even unpredictable in word and action, I showed him daily the way to the divine food. With constantly examining look to the back I had to make sure that he also followed me, however, in the hall he turned in the direction of sitting room and then went on the terrace.

»Eye masters, the kitchen lies in opposite direction,« I meowed to him behind.

On the terrace he looked to the sky, in the infinite width of the world-spatial panorama. However, what is to be seen there? A few clouds, a sky, whose colors vary depending on weather conditions. A few birds flying back and forth and are in search of food.

Up there they play even with building blocks. Fill, nevertheless, for the moment the feeding bowls, then you can further draw inspiration from the sky, I imagined than I saw quite intensely to him.

Suddenly I see as a smile creeps on his face as he began to smile slightly. Probably my thoughts are unexpectedly hiked to him, without having to say big words. We may have also thought purely coincidental to the same.

Master went forward at least in the kitchen and prepared breakfast for us everybody. Then he went with his coffee mug again on the terrace and sat down in one of the garden chairs. However, I had to clear off to strike my neighborhood which waited ready with a wide grin and treats for me.

When I came about midday again home, master was not there, was probably occupied to buy feed for us. Rex slept in his hut and thus I also lay down for sleeping on the chair, on the masters still sat this morning.

Sometime I woke up from to the bruit this open to the terrace door, jumped from the chair and ran in the house to see after the garbage amount of my feeding bowls.

Master came behind, opened his post, got immediately bad mood, became crimson in the face and caught in to grumble. Then he took a flask of schnapps and a glass, sat down and caught in to drink, in this time.

I remained nearby to pay attention to him, seemed in such a way that the post had sent him no good news. Master was already so sad some days ago, maybe a connection exists there, and I do not know it. In not too wide distance I lay down and observed him how drank further as he poured out over and over again in his glass.

It must be something depressing that bothered him so. I was afraid, afraid of losing him, but because he once said he had to go to jail. He cannot get me to leave you alone, not after what we have experienced so far. I sat next to his legs and felt his hand caressing my skin. I took the full enjoyment, which gave me my master.

His friend came and together they blathered about the things which were strange for me about imprisonment, arrest, jail, about legal advisers, lawyers and offices, about judge, penal defender and advocates.

Master drank too much, already spoken by the nose, an uncontrolled one mumble and he on no account opened mouth far and acted thus, as if he carries a clothes peg on the nose. To talk an indiscernible kind which nobody understands to hear a complete sentence from indistinct mumbling and a little rest intelligibility out.

»You are got drunk something like that from,« mentioned Marc what master answered: »I am not drunk, I find all that only shits.«

»Come I bring you now in the bed,« meant Mac. »You are a good friend. If you know, intelligence drinks and eats stupidity.«

Marc had brought my master to bed, had still put to us feed and then has disappeared. I lay down in my little bed and dreamt.

I dreamt how I marched alone through the streets. I had no home, no friends, was put on myself alone. A garbage tonne stood in away. Around her around empty packaging, cardboards, paper, plastic foil, nothing eatable, besides. I went around the corner and remained are on the brink when the wind allowed rolling an empty PET bottle above my way.

When I went past to a building where shopping carriage bays stood, a sleeping alcoholic frightened suddenly high and tried to get up chaotically before himself cursing, however before he succeeded I was over for a long time in him.

Then I saw a thick fat rat and my abdomen caught in to growl. Immediately I ran to her behind here, because nothing is worse than to have hunger and nothing eatable.

We rest along the street. She is extremely quick if one considers the short bones, but with me in the nape this is clear. Then I would learn to fly even this.

On the next corner, I noted how our distance became smaller and smaller. She became weaker, could hold the long-distance run not by and it would not last any more long, until I have them.

Suddenly twenty rats bumped there, tried to circle me. A duct to me to the leather wants. It was a trap in which I have groped about unsuspectingly in. However, with a sentence I jumped about them and ran off. During the running I looked around, saw behind myself the pack following in a bigger distance. Meanwhile to me slowly the puff went out, they were still fresh and who knows how many mate about those still on me wait.

I ran back to the garbage tonne, hid under the cardboards, however, the rats cannot be disconcerted and tore the packaging in lightning-speed, until I appeared from a cloud of plastic, paper and cardboards again.

Visibly exhausted I jumped again over them, raced down the highly defective road. There must be a way to find where I can jump up to where rats give up the chase. A tree, no one tree they climb with ease up, but a wall that is so high that I can skip it. A goal would be of no advantage when they crawl under, though a brick wall, since rats need an eternity to come up. But where can I find here a mason, I can climb saving as.

My forces decreased and I saw how the distance became smaller and smaller like they caught up to take apart me. I could not run any more, the bones hurt me, dyspnea agreed, to me became almost dizzy and to me burnt the eyes of the wind, the mud, sand and rubbish which blew to me in the face.

With closed eyes I went on to me voices heard. Uncertainly and step by step I opened my eyes. I looked around and noted that I lay in my little bed. I was a home with my family and all other was only one dream, a bad dream, and a nightmare.

Again I heard the close voice from little woman how she spoke with master how she tried to persuade him affectionately.

Meanwhile I went to the kitchen to see after my feeding bowls. They were there still. Then I went to the bedroom, saw like little woman and master on the bed sat and pleased me to see them. They were more welcome than ever, I had a home and friends for life, my little woman, my master!